ET--BEINGS 4

Man's Extraterrestrial Ancestry Transitions
(MEAT)

By: John Q Zarr

This book, like all my ET-BEINGS' books are dedicated to those who are seeking the True

WHAT IF?

and

Especially Margie, my soul/star mate whom we have been together in many times and many forms and rolls to each other...

What IF we can come around many more times together...to share more, and to learn more, and accept more from all the Universes/Time Realms...

WHAT IF???

I guess I need a "disclaimer here" This is listed as a book of fiction as all my ET-BEINGS books, DVDs, and/or classes; and since any of the main/or sub-characters can not be claimed as real or not there should be no confusions with real people. And since several major organizations of the world seem to have a very active denial process about characters and subjects I write about don't exist, and this appears as autobiographical and the conversations can not take place... then I feel I have a very strong disclaimer as to what is real and not real. However, any reference to any actually known person is strictly for reference only, and can be verified by multiple entries on the Internet, other books and news articles etc.

Segments
Man's Extraterrestrial Ancestry Transitions
(MEAT)

ET--BEINGS 4

Man's Extraterrestrial Ancestry Transitions

Introduction to MEAT

Okay, let's get down to the "stew." The ole' potatoes and meat, and the thick sauce of it all. Transitions, tangents, interceptions/interactions with the human species evolutional development within certain parameters of time and space.

What IF, the ET-BEINGS knew what our and their futures were going to be like?

What IF, the ET-BEINGS knew that because they had/have the technology to manipulate time and space events that "had and will happened?"

What IF, the ET-BEINGS knew that they were going to be an ET-BEING species that they did NOT want to become in order for man-kind to survive extinction from totally within internal germ-warfare?

What IF, the ET-BEINGS knew that man-kind "beginning" existence on the new primitive planet (earth), ***would not exist for another 9,100+ million years*** (give a few +/- 1,000 years)?

What IF, the ET-BEINGS knew the human species would not follow the set evolutional path from its beginnings to become the human species that it is now?

What IF, the ET-BEINGS knew unless they interfered at a specific time with certain DNA gene manipulations that they as future humans would never exist as well?

What IF, the ET-BEINGS knew that unless the terrestrial (as in the planet Earth), ET-BEINGS did not become our founding ancestors and intervene as "good parents" and conceive and "protect" the off-spring from all other entities interferences, the human the homo sapiens species would become a non-advanced homo erectus due to natural evolution?

What IF, the ET-BEINGS knew there would an astronomical number of What Ifs that would happen, and need answers as the result of the terrestrial ET-BEINGS intervening in both man-kind's and ET-BEINGS joint/dual dependency conceivement, development, histories, futures, and survivals?

****

MEAT! ... Why MEAT?

Flippant answer...there used to be a commercial about "Where's the Beef?" The hamburger commercial made this "little old lady" an over-night sensation. Also aren't there people who believe the space aliens are going to "eat us" just like we feel we have the "right" to grow/harvest cows, pigs, chickens, and a vast list of what we consider sub-species for our carnivorous nourishment/enjoyment? Aren't we "sub-species" to the "extraterrestrials?" Shouldn't they have the right to the same behavior as we have towards those we consider insignificant sub-species...to devour us at their leisurely delight...just like we do others?

How about when we say or someone says "you are going to eat those words." Or, the "taste" of crow?"

In this case re-read the title...Man-kind (that's supposedly us), Extraterrestrial (that is normally thought of as "outer-worldly"), Ancestry (that is normally consider our elders), Transitions (that is normally (from the dictionary)): "movement, passage, or change from one position, state, stage, subject, concept, etc., to another; change: such as...the transition from adolescence to adulthood...and many more "changes even in music."

As I said, "the natural evolutionary chain of events would only slightly modify the Homo erectus." The possible intervention of the evolutional change of the Homo Naledi may provide some valuable incite into the development of modern man. Do the research yourself...compare HN to the information on the physical stature of ET-BEINGS in almost all recalled encounters with small beings etc,, etc., and etc...as Yule Brenner says in the "King of Siam."

I've included a very small sampling of the Homo Naledi information to give the reader something to chew on...instead of a hamburger or pencil erasers.

Scientific classification e   Order: *Primates*

Suborder: Haplorhini   Kingdom: Animalia

```
Phylum:     Chordata          Family:   Hominidae
Class:      Mammalia          Genus:    Homo
Infraorder: Simiiformes
                  Species:   H. naledi
```

See anything interesting in this listing?

I don't really need to write a lot about all the What Ifs that I previously listed or others...those were covered in detail in the other books and classes. The correlation to man-kind and between the ET-BEINGS is what I want you to see. When a vast amount of things is THIS SIMILAR is IT really an Accident or COINCIDENCE?

****

Birth of Earth and Dinosaurs

Let's estimate the earth is approx. 5.65 billion years old, and the "first" recognizable species was sort of primitive fish that came around ole let's say 5,000 million years ago. Contrary to the thinking of my young nieces and nephews that was a little bit before my time. The earth was a "hot boiling" place that produced a lot more global warming effects/gases than we have now. That was mandatory for the terra-forming to take place.

According I think to science experts these life forms were not single one cell ameba's or what have you, but actual entities that hunted, ate, reproduced and died and made room for more evolutional off-springs. However, I'll give the devil his dues that these primitive fish may have in all likelihood started out as single cell animals that divided (multiplied), and eventually grew into these primitive little "fishies." Sort of like gigantic Piranhas, but nothing like the fish in the Amazon that eat Piranhas for fun (the *Arapaima,* also known as "pirarucu" or "paiche")," this sucker can weigh upwards of 90 pounds and has hard-plated scales.

Also here is a good time to remind you that TEACHER and her kind are NOT the only visitors to earth. They don't talk to me and I can not swear that **"they"** did not do some interfering with earth's evolutional progression. So don't blame me or the messengers... according to TEACHER they (the non-family others), interfered with her kind plans as well; and they had to do some quick manipulations and modifications here and there, or what us geeks call "tweaking with a crowbar and hammer."

Since I was not technically there, nor was TEACHER, or the Elders this is all speculation with what hopefully, will be logical answers...and I want to save some time by presenting the gist as in logical Q/A...for example:

1). From the beginning to the end of the dinosaurs, (however, millions of years), since TEACHER and her kind can travel back/forward of this time line they knew present day man would be relying heavily upon hydrocarbon products. Logically, the big trees forest, veggies, flowers and dinosaurs would need to be BIG IF all that hydro-carbon demand was going to be required. It made no logical sense to have itty-bitty animals and plants have the responsibility to die, get pressurized, and transfer into crude now would it? So, the bigger the better and yes, ladies size Does matter☺>

2). Speaking of size, the idea of the brain of a dinosaur is about size of a large walnut or small lime is crap. That is not logical when you look that the skull and eye sockets of....let's say T Rex...here is an average 7 Ton eating machine that is cunning and quickly adaptive to its environment and preys locations. The T Rex brain needed to be the size of an ape, a big adaptive ape, such as a gorilla not some liver fluke flunky. This size comparison needs to be logically adaptive to all the dinosaurs, and just because you had a massive body like the Dreadnoughts who basic eats plants but had massive teeth that replaced themselves every six months or more often had a brain the size of a cat's. But when that big thing died and got cooked and pressurized it produced a few dozen barrels of "black gold."

3). POOP! Yep caca stinky big globs of the stuff was full of what was eaten and when that got cooked and pressurized it produced hydro-carbons, too

When it came to making hydro-carbons the earth spared nothing in its giant highly pressurized cooker... while here and there it made a few really nice diamonds, too.

Did anyone/THING interfere (or "tweak"), with the evolution of man...the species? Missing links as in a let's say a "chain." Remember, in the other books the "Bloodline" causes a LOT of interactions between us the human and THEM.

TEACHER and her kind are basically "nice," even with the no deviation from the mission requirement compared to the other "visitors," especially the three fingered ones that are divided into two ranks. The taller ones are the bosses per se' and the shorter ones. These usually are the one's who interact with their targeted abductees (I use abduct because it is that...a lot more "intense" than with TEACHER and her kind.

As I said, "The bloodline often-times determines a lot of the interactions and extent of the interactions by any of the "Interactors." There is no dibs, sanctuary/"hands-off" on bloodlines, as far as any interactor is concerned. The DNA or source of information or physical "contribution" is up for grabs by whatever grabs you first, second, third and so-forth.

And the True Greys are at the top of the abduction food chain!

However, luckily (so-far), they interact with the human less than all the others at any given time. Never-the-less when **they** do interact with the human, IT is usually the most intense deepest embedded/longest lasting result driven encounter.

I am not going to go into a lot of details about encounters, interactions, abductions, or out-right stealing a person, because I have written so much about it my other books and so have a lot of other authors...some who seem to know something, and others who don't know nothing, and love to pontificate and expound their stupidity on those they perceive as lesser/unworthy

Ponderations?

Mankind may manipulate some of others technology to produce all these different UFO sightings episodes around the world because mankind is primarily using or abusing the less secure technology that has either actually crashed (very few have ACTUALLY crashed), or the staged crashes to give mankind military access to old technology to others, that is very new to us.

We cannibalize the technology from what bits and pieces our infantile brains can comprehend (like transistors, chips (not talking about LAY's) etc.), that are "gifted" to us by implanting an idea into the proper brain wave receiver, and then we proceed with the testing development and then wah lah we have a new "disruptive technology that seems to be a "miracle advancement way-a head of its time."

There are so much convolutions in these UFO reports and events produced by them, they and others I am not going to even try to present the truth about staged incidents, so-called abductions by little green men, or heavy set/square jawed dudes wearing sunglasses inside (sunglasses that are huge and cover a lot of the eyes/face), or all that other BS that we are handed/told it is for "our own good/protection." Yep, and I have ocean front property in Arizona (might if California breaks off into the Pacific).

I'll probably close this segment here by asking this logical question...

Where would present day man be in the evolutional chain of timed progressions if there were no interventions? What IF TEACHER and her kind did not have the technology to travel and document man's development? Would there be a "present day man-kind/" Would there be a "future day man-kind" in a form of TEACHER and her kind.

What If neither developed? What IF it wasn't TEACHER's Elders who made the evolutional change in man-kind's development...What IF it were the GREYS?

****

Six Fingered Hand...actually 5 fingers and one very unique thumb and other "neat stuff."

The development of the 6 digit hand on TEACHER and her kind is so very important. Remember where I wrote "pi" plays a very large part of their lives. Well, just because the Mayans had a 364 degree circle did NOT make them correct in the correlations of many harmonics of the universe.

Let's live with assumption that a circle is 360 degrees. The 6 digit hand has this laid out as 60 individual integers per digit on one hand and 30 integers per digit on two hands.

Remember in ET-BEINGS 1 A Report On Extraterrestrial Communications **"THEY ARE SEGMENTED INTEGERS**...." Well, now you know why it was said.

The dual stereoscopic eye sees everything in projected 6 perspectives as described in ET-BEINGS 2 A Textbook UPDated. The normal "X/Y/Z axis and the center point of each XYZ axis interceptors. These six dimensional observational points are automatically interpreted in the brain just like we see everything upside down and the brain flips it over so it makes sense. But the focal point on the macula from the lens is inverted. Same for TEACHER and her kind but only it is reflected as the drawing shows off a reflective inner lens before the image reaches the brain.

The six digit hand has a direct relationship to what the ET-BEINGS sees and how this corresponds to pi the what seems to be the never ending numerical number of circles. You may be asking how is this true? It is all primarily a supposition based upon what I've "absorbed" from being with TEACHER and others of her kind, and as far as our "old modern day history," it can easily be traced back to old Egypt/Pharos and false Gods.

As far as that goes so can a lot of the so-called "secret societies," and how they got their different/similar beginnings. I am not going to write a lot about them as there are massive amounts of books, documentaries, films and stuff written about them already. I am just showing you correlations.

Islamic 6 is also important as in the #6 is very important number in the Islamic religion, and how that correlates to the #9. Those correlations are based upon the moon, cycles and times both terrestrial and sidereal. I am not going to write a lot about that either for the previously stated reasons, again just correlations. I am not writing this to give you fluff...but stuff without the fluff.

SIX DIGITS EQUAL EXTENSIVE SECURITY PROTECTION:

What do we humans with our five digit hand and the ET-BEINGS six digit hand have in common? Lots actually as far as physical and adaptively uses of the "opposing thumb on our present day man, and the unique slightly modified opposing thumb of the ET-BEING.

Well, for one thing (not covered in **ET-BEINGS 1 A Report on Extraterrestrial Communication, or ET-BEINGS 2 A TEXTBOOK UPDated**), we all have some form of "finger prints or digit prints. Whereas ours are all different curves and circles that does not really identify us as by name etc., until we get into a finger-print data base somewhere and there is a record that can be scanned and retrieved with a fairly certain amount of probability accuracy. Whereas the ET-BEINGS' finger or digit prints are much different per se.'

The circular print does have a very basic design to ours however it is an ID system that primarily identifies the cloned or cloning family. TEACHER and her kind within her family not hive have the same circles with what looks like ridges and crosses that identify her cloned family. All her digits and those of her family all have virtually the same identifying "finger print" on each digit and each hand. The only slight modification is one small area that is mission Identifier such as TEACHER, a communicator and others that have different identifying mission requirement jobs within the family and hive.

And as stated the six digits assist greatly in security of not only the star ship operations but also in the personal control of the sleep modulators, food replicators and even the purging of "un-needed stress due to emotional deprogramming." I'll get more into that specific area a little latter.

Again, one area that is "frustrating" to virtually all other species is the security protection that six digits gives TEACHER and her kind. The controls of the star cruisers use six digit controls. The six digits are damn difficult to duplicate for man to use the technology as well as others who are a lot more technologically advanced than we are...especially the 3 digit dudes.

RIGHT HAND

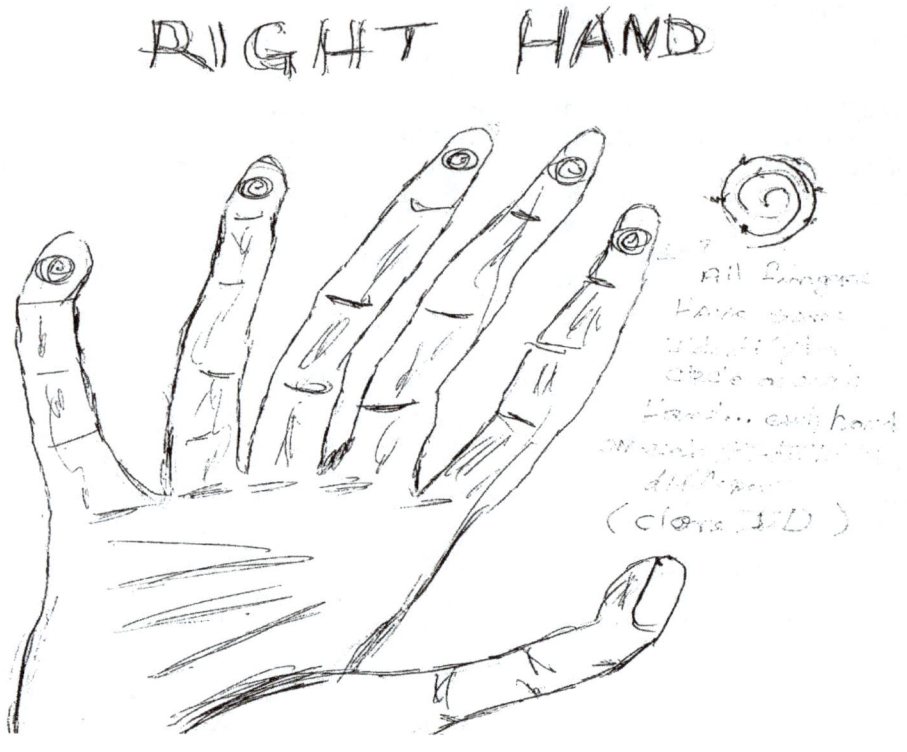

SIX DIGIT HAND (TEACHER'S): All fingers/digits have the same swirls with markers. All 12 "finger/digit prints" are the same and identify the cloned batch. This is how the "family of TEACHER" is identified, but not the hive. The Hive is composed of other families and they have different identifying swirls and markers for each family.

****

LOOPS NOT HOOPS THERE'RE TUBES...

Remember, when I talked originally about all those tubes? I never really went into very much more detail except they were "whitish looking"...at least back then the appeared whitish. I really don't think the color is important except that they may be whitish looking because the swirling liquid was composed of a modified mercury, silicon (lubricant), and Palladium (for mass/weight), and conductivity of electricity (electrons).

The swirling white hot ball of liquefied electric "jello" that has fried ET-BEINGS when it got away from the magnetic shields is powered by these gyroscopic liquid generators. The entire space disk vessel is one big swirling magnetic power ring within another within itself.

Gravitation bands of pulling force are neutralized by these magnetic swirling rings of electron forces. Especially, when they vibrate at a frequency that was totally undetectable to me at the time. I never realized the tubes were vibrating at a very high frequency because...to be honest this to me was my first "encounter" and I was a scared shitless KID! Remember that round room...well there's a brown spot and yellow stains on that round room floor somewhere.

Logically, present day man would not normally believe you can produce nearly a trillion watts of electricity with swirling magnetic fluid, oh, but you can.

Just think how a generator works now...a conductor moves through a magnetic field collecting electrons, and those electrons go to something that demands the electron feed (power etc.). Got it...understand it? NOW think like an ET-BEING!

BLOCK Hard headed, square jawed square brain think only inside the box present day man-kind says you can only get a certain amount of power from a conductor intersecting a fixed magnetic field at a certain speed/time. That is true, and as long as the experts all agree to that, then that is all you are going to get....and it serves man-kind right that is all he gets because he can not pull his "intelligent head out of his dumb ass unless everyone says it's OK to pull out." You can quote me on that, if you like, or not.

But what happens when the magnetic filed is not fixed and nor are the interceptors...only the collectors? Use a 1/10,000,00s more of the brain the Great Creator gave us. WHAT IF the swirling fluid was all magnetic, and what if the vibrating tubes were all interceptors? What IF the interceptors all vibrated at perpendiculars to the swirling magnetic field? How much voltage could you produce?

I am going to leave that right there...sorry if you do not get the idea with all that I said. I am not going to draw you a detail picture of how everything works. I will say this....TEACHER told me someone who read this started experimenting with what I wrote, and took almost everything I said verbatim and made the first hyper stellar drive prototype. It did not reach the speed of light but it did reach over 1,000 times faster than any standard liquid fuel fire cracker/roman candle rocket we have now.

WHAT!....WHY?...TEACHER says, I have to include drawing(s) to make sure the researcher that "discovers my information" is documented to commercial use according to the recorded future/history data recorded date.

You must be kidding? Yeah... yeah, I know you don't joke....jezz TEACHER what a pain in the ass you can be sometimes. Ha Ha very funny...Remember you are NOT supposed to have any emotions! What do you mean it's not emotional...**IT IS LOGICAL.** Reader, please pardon me while me, myself and I have a private conversation with TEACHER.

Okay, I'm back...she said, "that I am doing very astutely at writing and having a 5 way conversation at the same time." I think she was being sarcastic at my statement of about me, myself and I. Never-the-less...

Reader, I know it sounds like I am lecturing you... me, myself and I am sort of sorry...I feel I have earned that right. I am technically an old curmudgeon that demands my damn senior discounts... What's that Teach...yes, you are older than I am.

WHAT IF it only reaches 500 times faster???

What's that you say...the drawing looks good but I need to label it so it is understood better. Do you want me to wipe their noses for them too?

Okay, I understand about the time line and the mission. How about I show both at the end of this segment, and let the researcher person decide if they want "hints?" Glad, that meets with your approval.

Considerations: If you take any of my classes or purchase my DVDs on ET-BEINGS WORLD and especially the workbook that goes with the classes and/or the DVDs, then you will review a much deeper presentation to the significances of all these different correlations and if they were products of well-timed/well intentional interferences?

I'll leave it up to you to decide if a "nudge" here or there within the entire homo-sapien's evolutionary history could affect the physical, psychological/sociological status of our development?

HUMMMM? Are we created to be what we are today...or tweaked to be something else.

What IF we (present day man-kind), were tweaked or NOT...what would we be today?

****

SWIRLING MAGNETIC POWER TUBES: MARGIE Generator....

Margie's spirit asked me to explain the MARGIE generator here because she said, the idea is copyrighted and protected by those very strict laws. I think her little pugged nose spirit might a slight ego complex, since she knows I named this totally revamped/technologically disruptive design in generator operations, performances, and efficiencies after her.

Both she and TEACHER said the swirling magnetic power tubes are very complex and convoluted to get the full scope of from today's tech minds. Plus since both Margie's spirit and TEACHER already know I have built a working model and tested several times and it PROVED to be almost 50% more efficient at producing MORE power than any standard generator they said it would make understanding how the swirling magnetic power tubes work and should lead to development within the time frame that TEACHER and her kind need to take place.

Yes Margie I will include drawings of the Magnetic Amplified Rotating Generator Increasing Energy (MARGIE) generator. What's that TEACHER you say...Yeah, it probably will help explain a little about how the basics of CMET/Mono-Polarity works, and why I call it CMET Mono-Polarity.

TEACHER, can I have some fun with those people who like challenges and/or puzzles? Yes, I want to present swirling magnetic power tubes first before presenting the MARGIE generator.

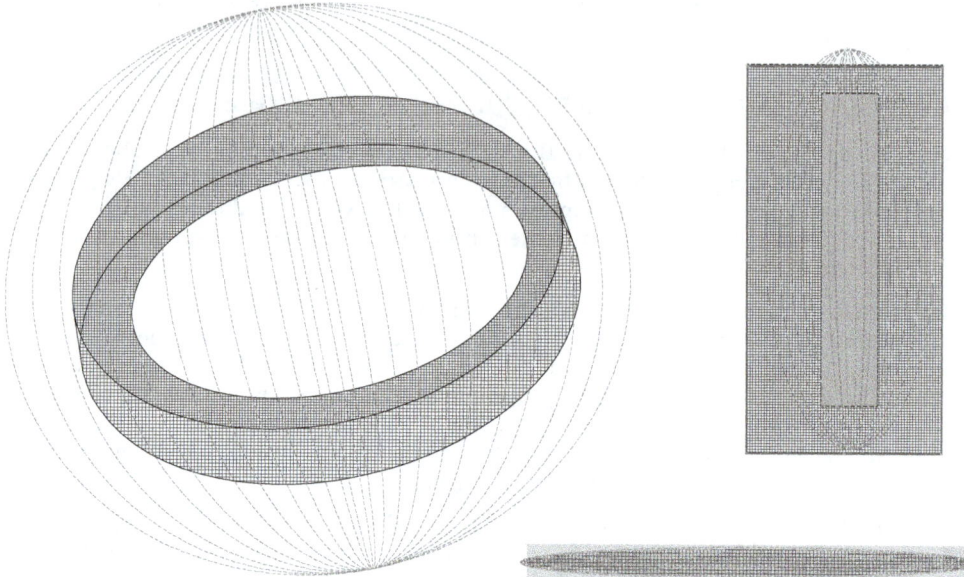

SWIRLING MAGNETIC POWER TUBES: This the non-labeled magnetic power tubes that are throughout TEACHER and her kind star cruisers. Based upon briefly what I wrote explaining how they work you may choose to figure it out on you own...if you respond to really neat challenges.

Don't "cheat" yet...Imagine your pride in yourself if you can understand this or even greater self honor/pride in being able to build models or 3D animated computer simulation without looking at all my notes including CMET/Mono-Polarity reports.

Never-the-less the "helpful notes and drawings" follow to assist you...the reader, researchers, developers, and investors. I will say that the "rate of return" could be astronomical.

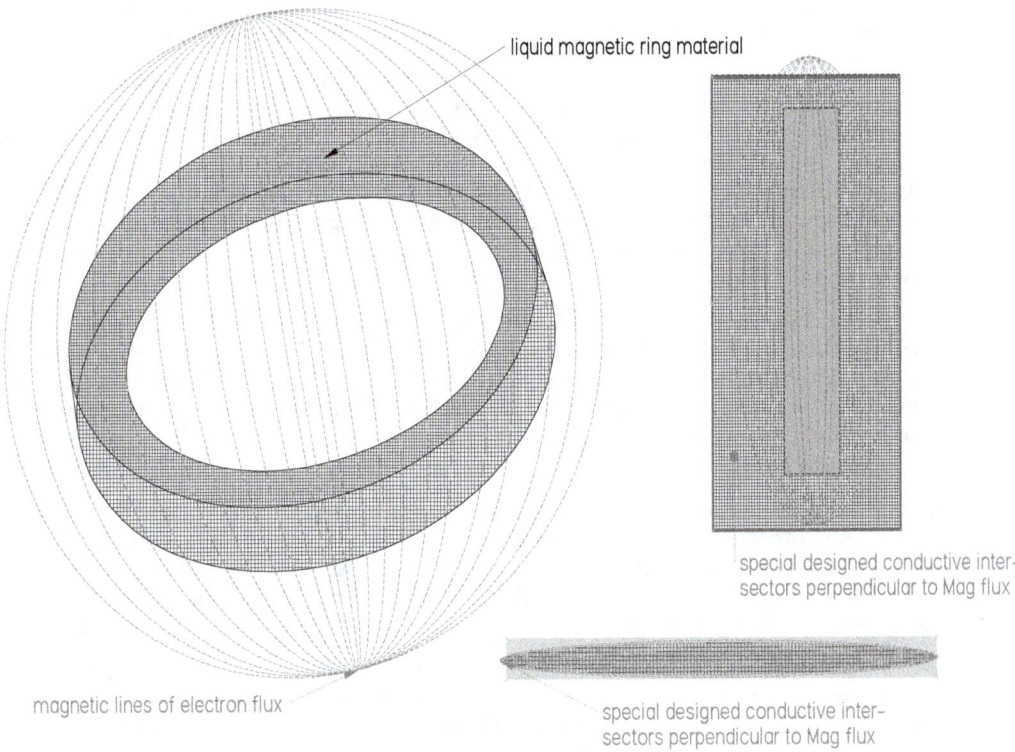

liquid magnetic ring material

special designed conductive inter-
sectors perpendicular to Mag flux

magnetic lines of electron flux

special designed conductive inter-
sectors perpendicular to Mag flux

SWIRLING MAGNETIC POWER TUBES 2B: How does it work? Well, since this is for man-kinds' supposedly benefit according to TEACHER and Margie's spirit both (me, myself, and I feel ganged upon), want me to go into detail explaining how these magnetic power tubes neutralize gravity and are a significant source of the tremendous amount of power needed to propel a star cruiser through time and the cosmos.

1).   The liquid magnetic ring inside the intersecter tubes is swirling at a tremendous rpm speed. Imagine a solid round magnet mounted to an insulated wheel being spun by a motor...except there is no motor, the tremendous gyroscopic force is driving the swirling liquid magnetic material. For experimentation you can use N-52 magnetic material. Magnetic slurry is not very old technology.

2). Design perpendicular intersecters that intercept and cut the magnetic lines of flux as it swirls by the intersecters. Increase the efficiency by making the perpendicular intersecters vibrate at a very high speed. Remember, the old magnetic law about the number of times a magnetic field is cut within a specific time frame. Well, you are now significantly "TWEAKING" that law...you are still using it, just on super steroids. I am NOT going to tell you how to design this vibrating perpendicular intersecter unit...use your imagination. Don't you want to have some fun doing your own work and design on this?

3). Collect the electrons on a collector plate very similar to electron collector plates now. With using a slurry of finely ground N-52 magnetic molecules you should be able to produce on hell of a powerful generator...especially if you design the vibrating intersecters properly. Even if you use the standard fixed intersecter grid and not have it vibrate to increase the number of intersections per fixed time, you will still have a very powerful generator.

4). Science presently is working on making vibratory reactions reduce the effect of gravity...so I am NOT going to tell you how to do that either, but it is simple if you just at what gravity (and light) are. IF gravity can bend light...then it is a force (FREQUENCY) that can be harmonized and then counter active to a near ZERO effect. Just think about it, one little segment at a time and work BACKWARDS!

Later! TEACHER is "pissed" in a non-emotional way. Listen, you have NOT ever had an argument worth anything until you have a disagreement with a being that does not have emotions. When you fight emotionally as all humans do a total logical creature; and you are bombarded with cold, hard, logical factual statements that hit you like boulders made out of lightning bolts you have Not had a good fight. Every time I opened my mouth I dug myself deeper into that hole that I was digging. Hell, Most times I didn't even need to open my mouth because both Margie's spirit and TEACHER read my emotional thoughts a head of time, and blasted me with my OWN logic. So here are some more tell-tell drawings to help you understand this swirling magnetic power tube technology....what? yes, I will also explain more of Mono-Polarity (later), and how this "un-shared" un-accepted knowledge is correlated to the basic operations of a star/time vessel...oh common on...give the hint of Relativity, black holes and "White holes" in time special planes. Geez TEACHER,....
Okay...Okay....I'll do some more explaining there, too. Now will you two please leave me alone long enough for me to figure out how may be I can draw this stuff, so the soft rocks can understand what this hard rock is trying to say?...Thank You...yes, we will talk later.

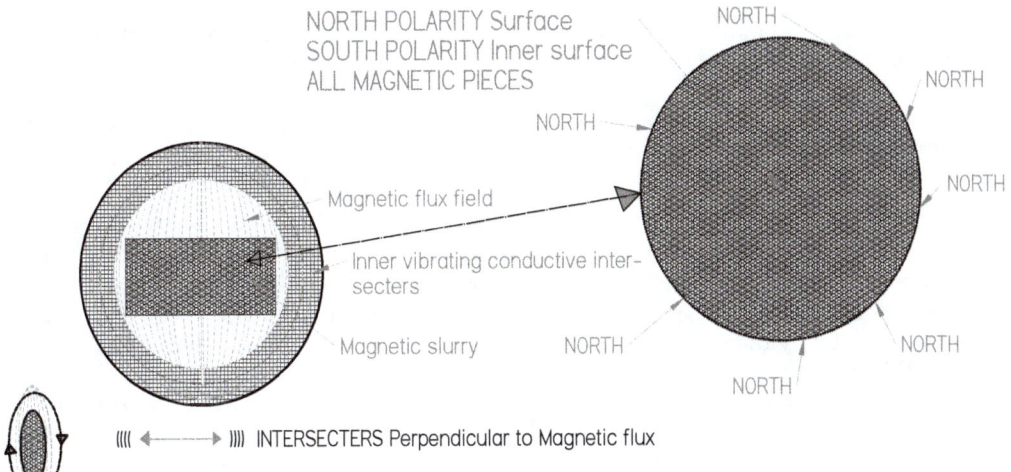

NORTH POLARITY Surface
SOUTH POLARITY Inner surface
ALL MAGNETIC PIECES

NORTH

NORTH

NORTH

NORTH

NORTH

Magnetic flux field

Inner vibrating conductive intersecters

Magnetic slurry   NORTH   NORTH

NORTH

((((◄──────►))))   INTERSECTERS Perpendicular to Magnetic flux

SWIRLING MAGNETIC POWER TUBES 3C: The magnetic slurry (represented as the rectangle), is actually round as shown in the close-up view on the right. This magnetic slurry is rotating inside the (PAY CLOSE ATTENTION HERE), perpendicular "rotating/vibrating intersecter tube." The inner wall of the outer tube wall is designed with a vibrator action that not only vibrates the intersecters, but, ALSO rotates the inner intersecters perpendicular to the movement of the magnetic flux.

This construction configuration produces a VERY SIGNIFICANT number of intersecter actions all within a very short span of time. With a frequency of even 1,000 hertz that is a 1,000 times more intersections within the same period that a single intersecter would cut a magnetic flux field. PLUS the perpendicular rotation of the inner intersecter wall adds a tremendous amount of intersections to the action as well. These actions take the power production capability to an entirely different and much higher efficiency level.

IMPORTANT INFORMATION: And if you have not figured it out by now, YES, these same technologies used today would dramatically improve all generators we use today. These technologies do NOT need to be on a star/time vessel but, can work right here today in utility power production, MRI, power sources--back up emergency power in disaster areas, deep in cold far reaches of out space, and actually **ANYWHERE WE USE GENERATORS TODAY!**

Some additional may be helpful information...get to know and understand everything you can about gravity. What it really is and what it really is NOT. Realize, that all mass has a gravity to a certain extent why? Holy cow, Teacher why do I need to tell very little thing I've learned over the eons? YEAH, I know...Knowledge not shared is a secret and there are no secrets in the universe only unshared knowledge...gezz...ok...what does dark energy mean to you? What is the charge of

dark energy? IF HYPOTHETICALLY speaking Gravity has a - charge and all mass has gravity then would it not seem logical that gravity has a pull or attraction to all predominate + charges...like earth, our sun or Alpha Centauri (what we call "grounded circuits")? So, are electrons and dark matter both NEGATIVE charged, and is that why they don't technically run into each other? Well, then if negatives repel how is it that electrons attract other electrons and produce different elements......THEY DON'T! Electrons are attracted to electron shells that are not balanced or have a missing electron that needs to balance. The rings are in need of balance and that is why electrons are attracted to other rings when there is an IMBALANCE. Read the proximities of Mono-Polarity....OOOOPs you can't it's a secret because I have not shared it, YET!

I am exposing the MARGIE generator under protest to Margie's spirit and TEACHER, but both said that present day human needs to get used to new ideas that challenge the general masses and a lot of the old laws of math and physics that have been ingrained and millions maybe billions have made their lives psyche/social status and even internal well-being.

They both say I need to be more non-judgmental and remember that no one else in the world has had the experiences that I have...just like being the first and only kid in the world to build an ION flying platform that earned me a NASA Space Achievement Award presented by Astronaut John Glenn (before his appointment to Congress). Plus the NASA award is signed by **Dr. Wernher von Braun** the first director of NASA. I also got a $10,000.00 grant...but that disappeared in the Viet Nam draft.

I don't know if you realize that since TEACHER communicates with me all these different 1,000s of times is in my mind and I have not been on a star/time vessel except when I specifically asked to be...and that is not very often because of all "safety precautions" that TEACHER and her kind need to do to ensure my physical, mental, emotional (remember Transporter Psychosis), and spiritual...my faith in the all powerful creators of all our universes, time realms and dimensions.

Just know and understand I do NOT talk or share a LOT of what has been shared with me. However, IF you have read the ET-BEINGS books (ET-BEINGS 5 is coming out very soon), or saw the DVDs, or taken my classes...I am sure logically you know I am letting you be a learning/sharing conduit that NO Other person has shared with you. Above all else you decide what IS and what IS NOT...if any...again where does the fiction and non-fiction divide...if AT ALL?

Okay let's look at the simple but totally kick ass revolutionary, disruptive Magnetic Amplified Rotating Generator Increasing Energy (MARGIE) generator and "discuss" all the little what ifs it has as it increases standard power production by close a factor of nearly 50% or more. Just by slightly lite touching tweaking I got 72% more power.

The laws we will be tweaking are magnetic laws that have been around for 100s of years and as I said so many people have adapted to man-kind's existence. These Faraday, Maxwell, Newton, Einstein, (and brethren Tesla), and 1,000s more were ALL on the right track and ALL made the MARGIE possible. I owe their dedication a great deal of appreciation...THANKS and may your spirits find favor with my endeavors.

Magnetic Amplified Rotating Generator Increased Energy

(MARGIE)

The Magnetic Amplified Rotating Generator Increased Energy (MARGIE), system/unit is an unique non-obvious invention that utilizes many well-known laws of science and physics to produce clean energy. However, if those well-known laws are "tweaked" to modify those laws can we actually increase the efficiency and/or performance of standard generators utilizing a common drive shaft. The premise of science is that you can-not get more energy out than you put in especially under no-load conditions. Never-the-less, can "thinking-outside-the-box" more power than previously is the dominate premise of energy production abilities? Note: I am not advocating producing more energy out than energy in however, I am advocating that more energy could be produced by "fine tuning" the premise of laws of magnetics by doing the following.

The Magnetic Amplified Rotating Generator Increased Energy (MARGIE), system/unit utilizes the laws that many respected sciences have discovered and a very important criterial of "conventional accepted proof". The first and most important is the number of times a conductor intersects a magnetic field within a specific time period produces energy by electrons being extracted from the magnetic field and collected upon the intersecting conductor. Faraday, Maxwell, and many others all have utilized and modified these power production laws to develop many of their well-known theories and scientific formula(s). Let's dissect this premise down to the minute segments that work in complimentary unison to produce power.

1. Conductors (usually coil), intersecting/bisecting (cutting through) a fixed/stationary magnetic force field produces a current by depositing an electron on the conductor.
2. The faster and the more a conductor bisects a fixed/stationary magnetic force field the more current produced (electrons are collected upon the conductor)
3. The power output is set to a specific or fixed time factor (faster plus number of conductors cutting the fixed/stationary magnetic force field is the law)

These well-known accepted laws of science/physic has been the premise to create generators, makes motors work and many more electronic operational circuits/systems work. However, What If the magnetic force field is not fixed/stationary at a fixed/set distance from the bisector? Let's look at the What If concepts…

What If the Magnetic Amplified Rotating Generator Increased Energy (MARGIE), system/unit utilizes the counter-clockwise and clockwise of bisecting magnetic force field at the same time, on the same common drive shaft within the same fixed time, will more clean power be produced as power out-put in relationship to the power in-put ratio? Please see the

drawings that helps explain these conceptual functions. What do these
conceptional drawings illustrate in a narrative format as an example:

The Magnetic Amplified Rotating Generator Increased Energy (MARGIE),
prototype model system/unit utilizing a common drive shaft that rotates at
a fixed rated 500 RPM. The fifty N-42 magnets are mounted in a conductive
shell (stator). The gausses rating (see spec sheet #1), of each of these
magnets at a fixed .35 inch distance between the magnetic surface and
conductor (air-space), is .62 pounds (9.92 oz.) pull force on a conductive
shell. Accordingly, the closer the intersector is to the magnetic surface
(air-space) the greater the beta force field. Assuming the drive shaft
rotating speed is 500 rpm and the 1:1 ratio of drive shaft/pulley system
the voltage out-put is 7 volts at .3755 amp (2.62850 watts). This "no-
load" 2.62850 watts power is produced by the 1,300 number of turns of 24
gauge magnetic copper wire coil rotating at 500 rpm within the previously
identified magnetic force field. The no-load out-put of 2.62850 watts are
the most amount to expect with all the para-meters are fixed/set.
However, this 1:1 pulley ratio with 500 rpm clockwise common drive shaft
is not utilizing any of the special conceptual "counter-clockwise"
capability of the stator that is "fixed/stationary" in all other
generators, but not with The Magnetic Amplified Rotating Generator
Increased Energy (MARGIE), system/unit.

The Magnetic Amplified Rotating Generator Increased Energy (MARGIE),
system/unit utilizes the unique ability of a round stator that rotates
upon wheels that allow the stator to rotate at one direction with a
"reverse" drive belt on a common drive shaft and a 1:1 ratio pulley drive
belt that rotates in the "OPPOSITE" direction of the stator.   This unique
configuration of clockwise and counter-clockwise operation actually
increases the number of conductive bisectors movement through a magnetic
field. This very unique and non-obvious clockwise and counter-clockwise
operation simulates the rotational speed (RPM), from 500 rpm to 750 plus.
The new counter rotational magnetic field effect rated out-put of approx.
7.64 volts at .4865 amps (3.71686 watts). Yes, it is less than the power
input (12 volts DC @.3450 amps= 4.14 watts), but the power output ratio
out-put is approx. 141.25% increase over the fixed no load wattage out-
put. This ratio change of 2.62850 watts to 3.71686 watts (141.25%)
increase over the fixed 500 rpm at no-load appears to actually increase
the power out-put/operational efficiency within fixed parameters.

Thus, the Magnetic Amplified Rotating Generator Increased Energy (MARGIE),
system/unit seems to be able to increase the power out-put expectations
utilizing the counter opposite rotational factors upon a common drive
shaft.

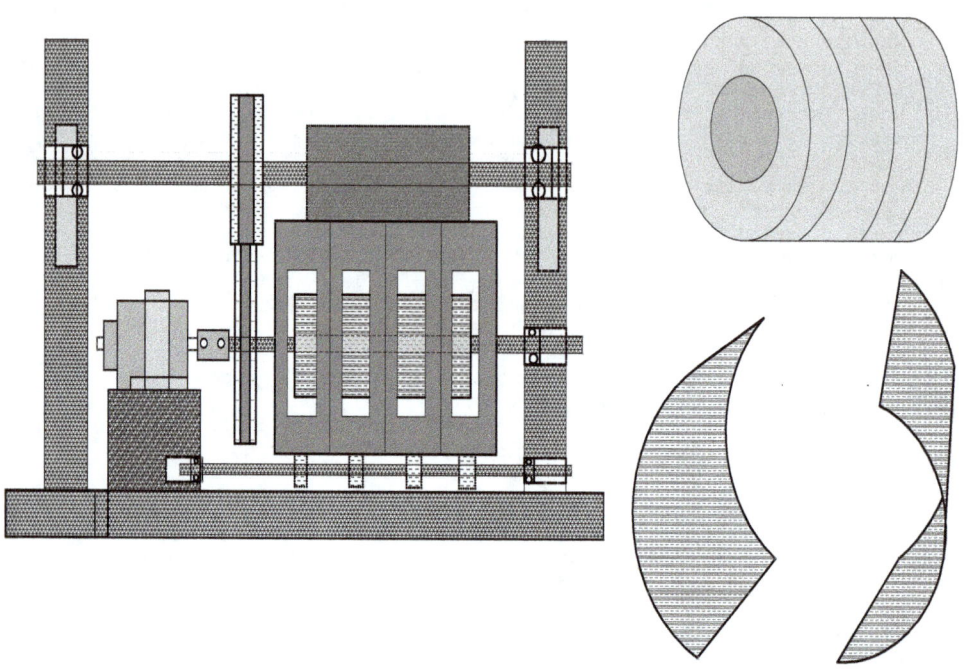

NOTE: Whenever you read and copy my invention's paperwork and copy it exactly you will copy and apply errors that I purposely put in there to try to make you fail. My little "warped" way of getting even with those who have a lot more funding than I do to do research and development, even to commercialization...so PAY attention to what you read and copy...you have been warned, and if it failed where it worked for me, don't blame me.

There TEACHER and Margie spirit communicator I have shared all I intend to share until PREMA **(ET-BEINGS 5),** is made, and she becomes PRETA (**When You See PREMA You See PRETA**), and NO! I am NOT going to label the parts. The very detailed explanation of what the MARGIE generator is and HOW it works should be enough for anyone to understand that is interested in building this and trying to PROVE me wrong. Remember, I built it...................................... and it WORKS!

I will be sort of be nice here and tell you a "way" you might want to look at how to make a swirling magnetic slurry...I'll give you a hint THAT WORKS (has worked for 100s of years), primarily the swirling is produced by the same laws that propel a mag-lev.

Oh crap! GEEEZZ!! Alright...I'll go into more detail about Mono-Polarity...later on Okay.

WHAT IF man-kind does not want to get to the stars, YET???

****

"T" could the "T" Represent TEACHER or Transportation?

What does that title mean? What technically does TEACHER and Transportation have in common to that question...and many more that will develop as you read, see, and hear more.

Another question is very important to the title is...what did Ben Rich (CEO/SkunkWorks), mean "we can take ET home and "WE" found an error in the equation." People may have thought he meant Maxwell's Laws from "Open Minds," Additional info: http://www.openminds.tv/lockheed-skunk-works-director-says-esp-is-the-key-to-interstellar-travel-video-1092/23042

Well, let's suppose that supposition was very accurate...where would that error be in the laws pf physic and magnetics that has been "utilized" so many years and by so many products and tweaked by so many inventors, researchers, professionals etc., including Einstein, Tesla, and so many more.

What could this "error" be... and what was the error... and **WHAT FIXED** the error?

Could it be **"MONO-POLARITY?"**

You ask what is Mono-Polarity? Well, there is a very thick book (written eons ago still probably back on that farm), that IS NOT published, yet including drawings, math formulas, and a lot more really proximity stuff that "TWEAKS" the laws of magnetics with two crowbars and a sledge hammer! And most people will need to be hit in the head with these finesse tweaking tools, just to get their attention, if they ever expect to "understand it and mercy me...accept it!"

Getting back to what Ben Rich said...ESP (no, not Extra Sexy Personality), but maybe the power of the mind? How would Extra Sensory Perception or ESP and magnetics propel a star ship? Well in **ET-BEINGS 1 A Report on Extraterrestrial**

Communications we played a little mental communication/teleportation mind game. Remember, when we went past the universe, or just to the corner store instantaneously in a "THOUGHT?"

What do brain waves and magnetics have in common? They are both energy! Okay, here is where we get out the TWEAKERS...where is it written by the Universes' really high level upper management dudes that "thinking yourself somewhere it can NOT be done...Is it NOT possible with IT ALL things are possible?"

TEACHER's words were...**" WHEN WE PERCEIVE THE CALLING OF THE UNIVERSE AND WE WILLINGLY HEED IT THEN WE WILL BE**... that is where I stopped quoting her. Now, I think we are ready to hear the rest of what she said...**THERE AS WE AND THE UNIVERSE DEEMED IT TO BE.** Ben Rich was being guided in his search for the What IF, and when he shared his statements with not only people at this seminar, but with the world in his open/public statements. All we have to do is hear and willingly heed.

So to share a little on the Mono-Polarity referred to in earlier writings. What is mono-polarity? As stated it is simple that magnetic single poles interacting upon itself. I know that goes against all the "known/Accept laws of physics, mathematics and magnetism as dual poles...but I ask you...Does IT really... or does it give greater definition to the behavior of the poles? What else has a duality (at a minimum)? Is not LIGHT an accepted duality....particles and waves? But let's be honest that so called duality is a LOT more!

LIGHT as a wave is frequencies, and frequencies are an integral part of the electromagnetic spectrum is it not...per se'? If we modulate the frequencies we also change the hues, intensity and the energy output do we not in a modified form of way?

LIGHT is also considered as a particle. This area has a little more "mystique" to it than modulating frequencies with a freq generator, pezo, or may be a quartz crystal.

According to the Mono-polarity notes when you take a slit wave test you get a rather unique series of events as to what happens when single waves/particles escape from the light slit. The light wave vibrates at certain frequencies and the wave length (hue) can actually be modulated by vibrating the frequencies of the light wave generator. Has anyone ever vibrated a magnetic field? Sure microphones and other audio devices do that, but what if it was on a much larger scale than the stereo headphones. What if it vibrated gravity?

OOPS the cat is running away from the sack, or something like that.

The Walls of Jericho came troubling down...Tesla vibrator machine no bigger than a small breadbox almost brought down the building that he attached to the supportive building structures the "earthquake machine." The "official police report claims that if he had not shut off the "contraption," when he did that the building would probably collapsed.

Trumpets can rupture the Hoover dam, and do a lot more damage...Have you ever seen explosive diarrhea from low frequency vibrations...not a pretty or sweet smelling scene. Talk about a "rumbling in your tummy." And remember the 2nd brain is in the GUT...Yuck!

Do you think a vibratory magnetic wave could be a force-field...how about a force field that repels gravity...man that cat is running like a scalded cat now. And with gravity out of the way or in more technical terms...neutralized as a holding glue...how far do you think you could travel and how fast.

Let's presume gravity is powerful enough to affect light...let's presume that something that is defined as a wave/particle can actually be bent by gravity tugging effect. OOOPs again another cat ran away because according to a lot of physicist gravity can and does bend light. Okay so that was an old cat...it still ran away before we fully understood what all the hissing, scratching, clawing and ripping that sack to shreds was all about. But, you should by now be beginning to glimmer a notion of what takes place, and may be even formulating a What If hypotheses.

Ben Rich also said..."It is ALL tied together." These are exactly what I have been saying/ writing about all these decades. The infinity figure of 8 and all its segments. Have you ever noticed how the Egyptian ANKH (symbol for life/eternal life etc.), looks like an eight with a flat bottom when standing. Never-the-less it is still an infinity (medical symbol), that is never ending/never beginning...no matter how many equal or unequal segments you divide it into.

WARNING: The following is taken from my research notes on Mono-Polarity. I will only share enough MEAT in the stew pot of Mono-Polarity to make you extremely hungry. I will say this I started Mono-Polarity before ET-BEINGS 1 was hatched. When I was a toddler/kid and TEACHER and her kind were "escorting" me through all the different phases of their existences...I am not sure if that was shortly before or after I drank that weird looking colored "Kool-Aid" that they gave me. However, I think I was pre-teen in years when I drank that stuff. Oh, now I remember a little more...I drank different stuff over a period of time...including a lot of my daddy's Old Crow and great-grandpas moonshine...long before I was 13. I do remember my first beer at the age of three...I don't even think they make Falstaff anymore? Tasted like water with a salty pinch...Can Not say that about moonshine...that was "tamed lighter fluid." I used it to launch my homemade rockets and blow up gopher mounds.

Short funny story... I remember getting pissed at my dad one time and I thought about putting the moonshine in the Studebaker station wagon, but I remembered how the home made rockets took off and the gopher holes exploded, so I decided I still loved my dad too much to see him "launched into space" flying down Hy. 79 in

Arkansas. I am not sure BUT, I think TEACHER pointed out the logic of not doing what I was thinking about doing. I wish she reminded me not to get my head so damn close to that 20,000 volt high amperage spark gap and I did not have to experience "seeing pain in my brain" as that spark gap burned a 3rd degree hole in my temple. However, I am very thankful for flying over everything in the workshop when that spark gap grabbed my brain; and I did not turn into a lump of burning putrid bubbling human "glooup." I still can not believe mother nor dad ever knew...thank goodness I had those extra black pair of "horn rimmed glasses" that covered the black hole in my temple. It was only about 1/2mm smaller than the glasses were wide and wild dark hair all helped cover the "mishap."

Being the idiot that me, myself and I am, I remember sticking a toothpick into the hole to see how deep the burned in ring in my head was...when I got to over ½ the toothpick was in the hole I figured I better stop...Hell what IF I punctured my brain (what brain I had left), with that damn toothpick! I never said, "I was the brightest kid in rural Arkansas."

MONO POLARITY and Me, Myself, and I with Tweaking by TEACHER

Time lapsed...I have been reviewing a lot of the notes I have compiled over the decades, and tried to remember my notes/observations that are back on the farm in Arkansas. I have after having several real heart to heart conversations with TEACHER that I will attempt to do the following concerning Mono-Polarity:

1).   I will write some really what I think are some WOW information about Mono-Polarity and why I call it CMET.

2).   I will also include the simple but very convoluted formula to how CMET (Mono-Polarity), works at the sub-atomic level

3).   I will include a drawing of CMET as "perceived" to function at some "NON-OBSERVABLE Point In Time" Because the act of observing obscures/ distorts the process.

4).   The most tricky.... I will try to locate my notes from where they are hidden on the farm, and I will attempt to publish the entire book on CMET/ Mono-Polarity, and as I said before, and in the book itself, I could care less if the world accepts it or rejects the concepts. My life, reputation, social status does not depend one nit, zip, nadda on the acceptance or rejection of CMET/ Mono-Polarity. However, by me publishing it, and USA Congressional/ Inter-national copyrighting laws NO-ONE can claim it, and it will always belong in the ME, MYSELF and I bloodline.

I'll try to make a color representation of a non-observable proximity event. The formula will be displayed as well. This formula is the entire meat, potatoes, onions and goulash of CMET / Mono-Polarity.

I will add the secret ingredients here that has been handed down through my spiritual bloodline for eons...and that goes PAST the time man was on this earth...does NOT mean he was not on other earths in different time realms and dimensions, and different form. Pay attention I am probably going to only say this about a 100 times in different ways.

What does, light, sound, gravity, earths, planets, constellations, our human cells, all living creatures, quartz crystals, and not realized YET time all have in common? Common think?

They all......................look at the last page☺>

CMET / MONO-POLARITY

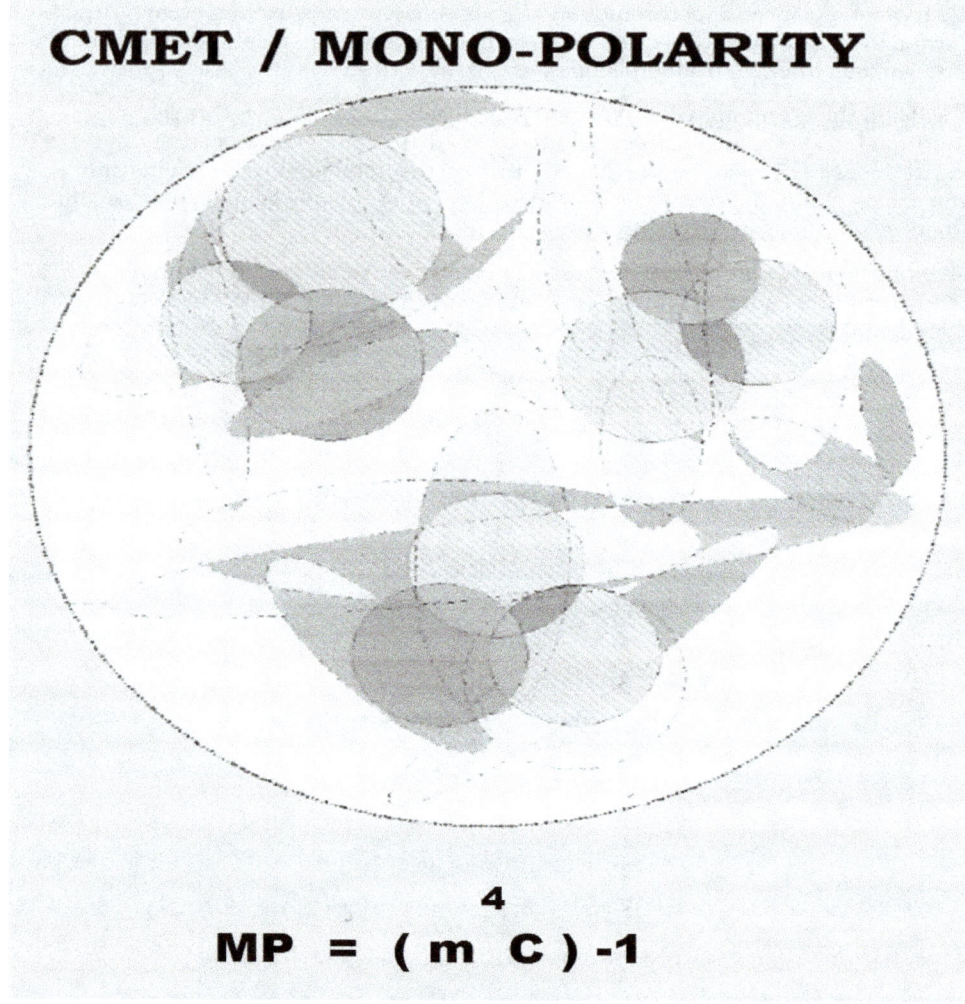

$$MP = (m\ C^4) - 1$$

Think about what that formula really means and represents in relationship to the known 4 stages of mass (solid, liquid, gas, plasma)?

WARNING: do not copy the information without testing it! There are "protective" errors (my/heir's protection), in the information...please Test, and RE-TEST and Verify. Remember this is NOT all my notes on Mono-Polarity.

PONDERINGS and HUMMMMMMM THOUGHTS?

Is it NOT agreed that the Magnetic North Pole a singular polarity with multiple applications.......

Is it NOT agreed that the Magnetic South Pole is a singular polarity with multiple applications......

Is it NOT agreed that matter is a single idea with multiple applications....

Is it NOT agreed that anti-matter is a single idea with multiple applications....

Is it NOT agreed that fusion is a single idea with multiple applications....

Is it NOT agreed that fission is a single idea with multiple applications.....

Is it NOT agreed that the laws of attraction is an idea with multiple applications....

Is it NOT agreed that the laws of repulsion is an idea with multiple applications.....

Is it NOT agreed that these laws are in constant need to seek balance with multiple applications.......

Do we choose to agree that all existence is a single mono-polarity in its most simplest form, seeking to be in all places at once within itself? Is itself all that ever be created?

Note: It is NOT important that my drawings are very clear or sharp...the most important is what they elude to. Such as, the slit light wave particle test. There are a lot of excellent examples all over the Internet...just look for them if interested.

CMET/Mono-Polarity is all about the hypothesis of " singular energy entities trying to be in the same proximity (location), of itself... **at the same time all at once."**

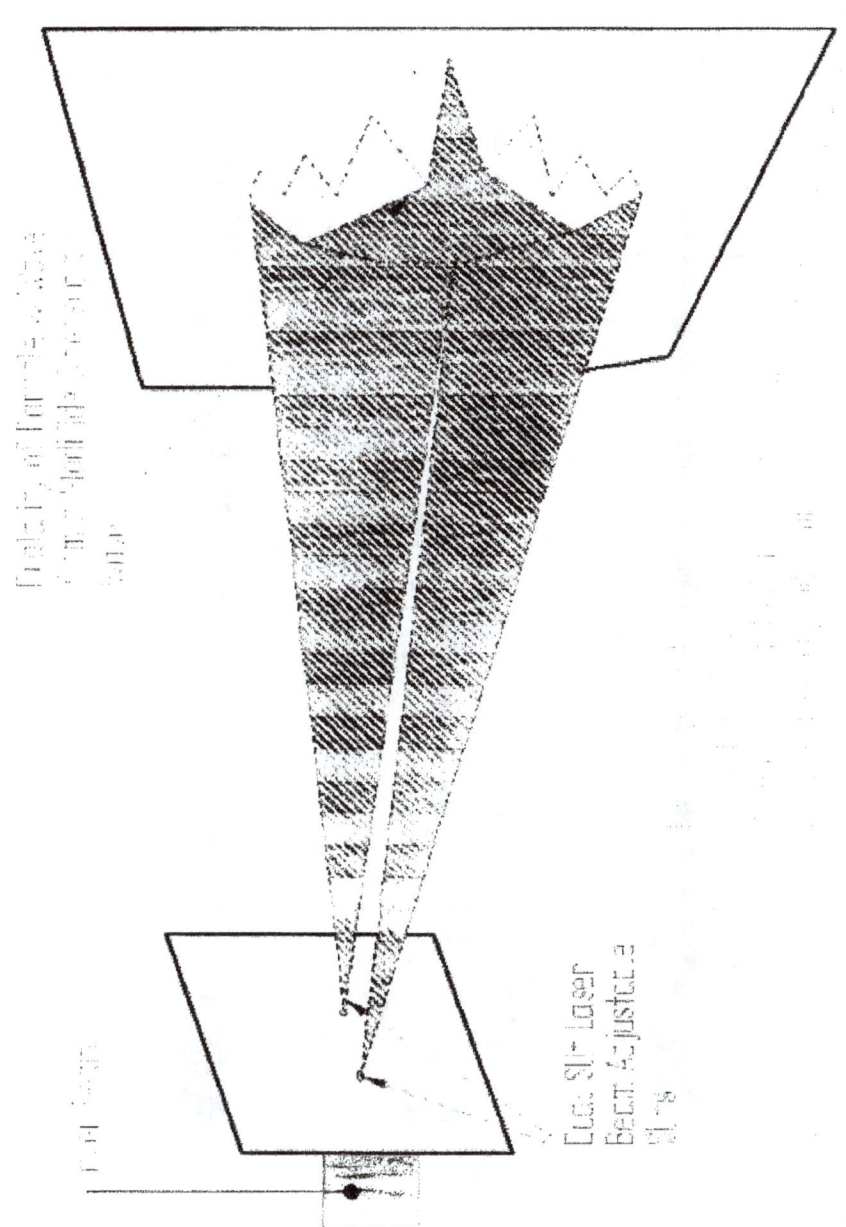

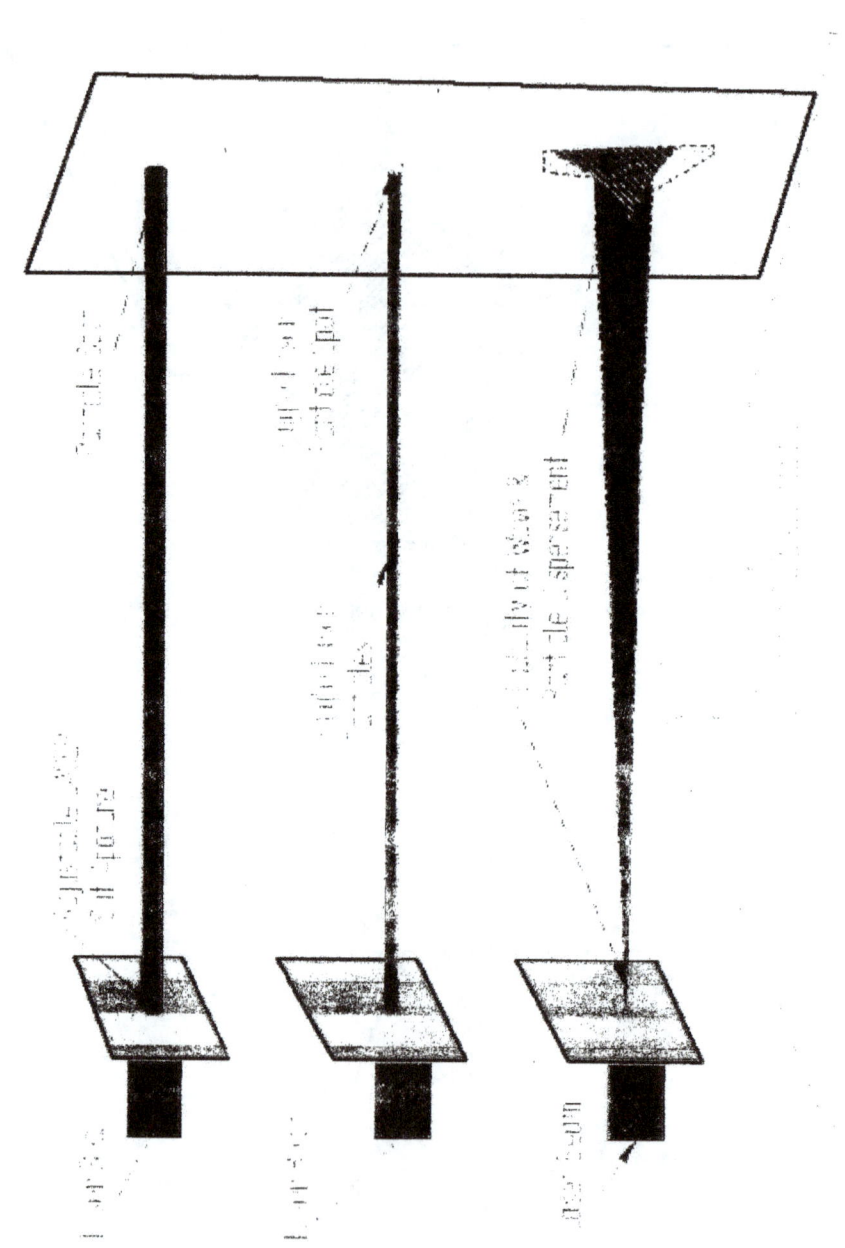

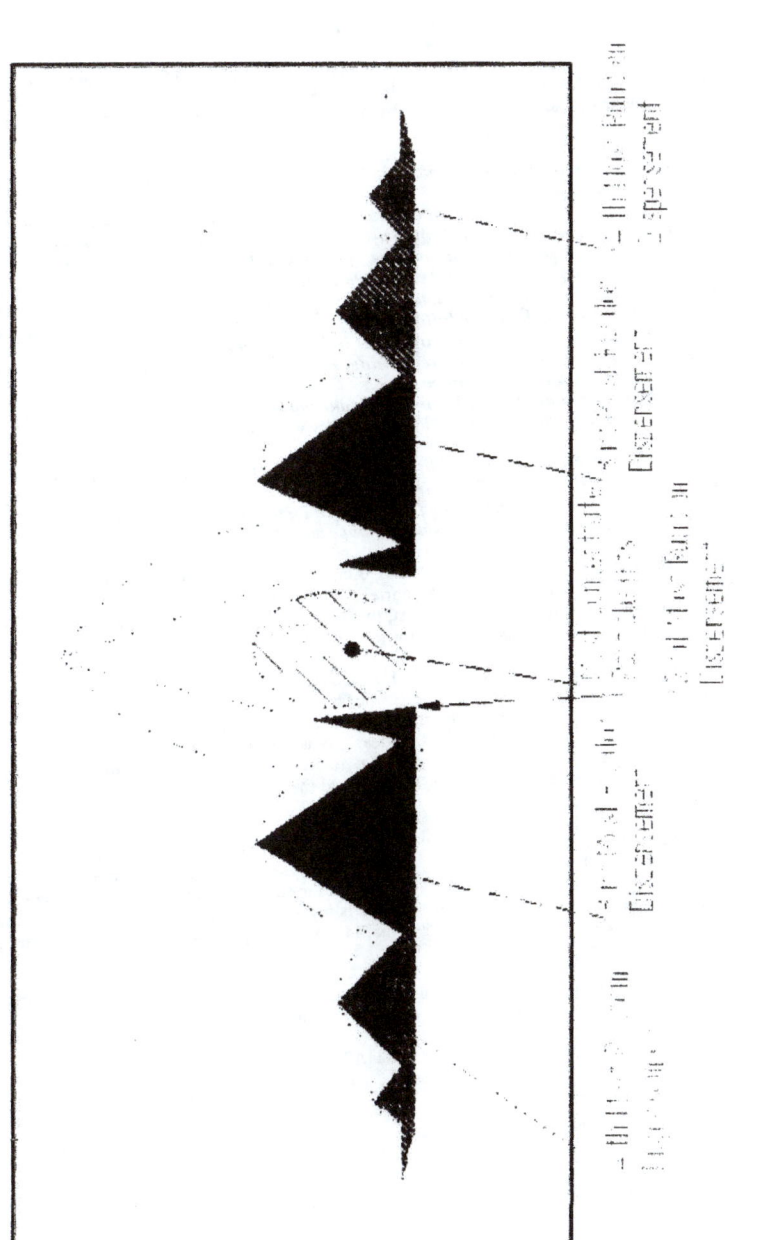

Mono-Polarity Perceptions

What is "Mono-Polarity Perceptions? In its simplest terms or definition is feeling and reactance of a mono-polarity entity behavior theorized, postulated, observed, and documented to fit within a designed reality. This can be a real or imagined reality for other observers to meet, greet, and share within and throughout the realities' realms of existence.

A friend of mine daughter just recent died while in Hospice. She said, "I always know what just to say." This is what I said…. " *Now,*

Ellie's (may not be her real name*), spiritual contract is full-filled….now is the time she receives her rewards for fulfilling that agreement. Her spirit begins to receive its rewards and also rest and awaits for another spiritual agreement to be made in a different time, space and different place and a different identity. Some of our spiritual agreements are longer and shorter than others, and some are easier on the spirit than others….there is nothing in these contracts about the vessel these contracts are fulfilled in and there is nothing in the contracts about how our fulfillment affects others physically….there is a spiritual collaboration of roles though….it is ALL part of our individual and collaborative spiritual contracts with each other and the Creator….all on that intertwining, never ending nor beginning ribbon of life…in ALL of its forms and times, space, and place dimensions….*
Be at peace you and your daughter's spirit fulfilled your portions of the contract beautifully…………….then I wrote a little more after she wrote and said "I always know what to say……

"I've thankfully feel I've have had several life existences, to TRY to get a glimmer of the truth…..I hope the Universe feels I still require a LOT of learning….before I can even come close to perceiving the truth….however, I have a sneaky suspicious feeling, once I get close to some answers, THEY will change all the questions……I hope so…for my spirit's sake….I hope so??????????

How does this relate to whatever Mono-Polarity is? Actually, mono-polarity according to many is an impossibility….it can not exist…..they may be correct in their assumptions. It is not important to me, if they are correct or not. I do not claim to be a physicist, theorist and my so-called reputation (whatever it maybe at any given moment), does not rest upon any of these assumptions.

If I have the opportunity to present this paper, and the whole world's learned elite boos the idea or presentation, I do not really care….okay maybe 10% of me cares…my spirit does not need the recognition this time around….I am not really sure presently, that it will ever need the recognition….Regardless, of the recognition, it does not change the thought of the idea….What IF there is a mono-polarity existence, and it is always seeking to be at all places at once? What IF there were a whole universe of mono-polarities, and they ALL were seeking to be in all places at once? What would that do to our perceptions, observations and documentations in our own realities?

Total empirical logic has always told us that all existence is at opposition and attraction of itself. We may not ever recognize nor accept this empirical logic…we as human's shroud our logic in an emotional cocoon. Emotional shrouding does not allow empirical logic. Could logic and emotion be the recognized or unrecognized Ying and Yang of all existences? If this is my empirical logic….does not have to be yours? It does not have to be anyone's, to make it real or unreal. Only the majorities belief in the perception can make it appear real or not…or does it.

Could it be, the What If of all existences in all universes, time realms, space and dimensions is the single opposition and attraction of itself? Is that what a Mono-Polarity is…………………………

WHAT IF

More info in the appendix

Celestial Monopolar Energy Transitions
(A Theorem of Effects)

It's been said, "That finding a mono-polar magnetic unit would be the science of Nobel Prize winnings," and it would be personally rewarding to be able to name it the "CMET."

The mono-polar unit would have to reside within a single space between the proton and neutron with balances equal to the total electron charge fog surrounding the atom. I am not implying that the monopolar unit be a single unit with a single counter polarity attraction to all the electron charge. There can be many, virtually unlimited monopolar units between the neutron and the proton of the atom, surrounded within the nucleus. The monopolar unit is functionally an invisible attraction glue, that not only attracts its counter parts but itself, into a subatomic slurry.

This attraction slurry is much smaller than the bonding shells that are known and theorized by science today.

Monopolar encasement is another way to look at it. The proton with its alleged positive(+) charge is said to be in suspension with its neutron counter part. Even though, the neutron by definition is "having no charge." However, it (the neutron particle) is theorized to be made from up and down quarks, and a host of other particles such as baryons, mesons, leptons, and others.

Thusly, the up-quark possessing one third the total weight and the down-quark having to balance the weight to energy ratio, has to have two down quarks making the remainder a two thirds ratio of weight energy equivalency. The up quark weight is one third more than a down quarks weight to energy equivalency.

At the sub atomic level, science sort of has to take a second look at itself; and that which holds true for the atomic and larger level or more expanded level of existence, is not the same laws at the sub atomic level.

Proximity is the slurry's adhesion to other proximities…or what I called changeling, or melding for a lack of a better term. Thus, we have the Celestial Monopolar Energy Transitions (CMET). Just like Celestial Miraculous Energy Technologies is the total big picture, the Celestial Melding Energy Temporal would be the atomic level, and the subatomic level would be the Celestial Monopolar Energy Transitions.

The Incredible Shrinking Man, movie/script message that some may have not understood was simply, no matter how small something maybe, its purpose is still a big part of the total universe. CMET explains it all.

Quantum Mechanics/Physics (QMP) is a science that is not true to the word "absolute." In QMP the supposition of the "What If" and the probability are the most compelling and definitive answers that one will get from the QMP world. The probability or the law of randomness (true randomness) is a factor of all QMP ideas or questions. However, there does seem to be a constant in the randomness…that energy probabilities do not really dramatically change from the standard physics and the quantum physics. Therefore, answers that would be derived by the hard and fast and logic factual world of non quantum physics (classical physics), will produce virtually the same answer within the quantum physics world as well.

The only difference is that formulas in physics such as speed equals distance divided by time is altered in the quantum world by random momentum surges and decelerations…or the variable of random probability, "of what if we speeded it up here and we slowed it down here, based upon a random picked grid." What would be the speed then? Surprising the segments when totaled would almost match the non random interfered with momentum. However, the segments (or the quantum random probabilities), would have different answers than a straight line of momentum, with no accelerations and no decelerations.

So, looking at quarks, baryons, and antiquarks and other subatomic particles in our proximity slurry we possibly may find that monopolar values are the only way the atoms' (nuclei/nucleus), stay together, and also meld into another element (giving/receiving electron charges), and still retain a portion of its original identity.

Monopolar slurry is defined from here forward as the adhesive attraction that sub atomic particles demand to be present in order to maintain stability that is always in motion.

It is NOT a force…it is the opposite of a force. It is the random probability of attractable proximity that this particle will want to pass through this area that is continuously perpetual to the time and space, and when it moves through (not to), that point in time and space it wants to move through another proximity in time and space. It never ceases its attractable movement. This process of attractable random proximity is in constant motion and activity for all particles within the nuclei, and the nucleus of the atom. The neutron wants to get closer to its proximity in time and space. The proton with its positive charges wants to get balance with the electron fog that surrounds it, and the entire atom wants to maintain order and adhesion to maintain its true identity.

It is this constant attractable "wanting" to be there when it is here, that makes all things possible.

Therefore, "proximity," is not exactly like what you thought the word meant, now is it… or as the Encarta English Dictionary (North American) defines it **prox-im-i-ty** (noun) = closeness in time and space. However, that implies there is a point of existence. A definite definitive location at a definite time with ONE reactant, and that one reactant is based upon the singular point and time location.

The absolute law that is not broken with a singular polarity is that being monopolar the singular likes repel and the singular opposites attract. However, there is this randomness of proximities that balances the singular monopolar attributes that because of constant momentum and randomness of singular energies that maintain this very delicate, yet very stable equilibrium of existence.

It is possibly this equilibrium of balance through true random proximity transitions that allow the photon to process the duality of a particle and that of a wave form as well. Shadows of photons (light) prove that it is a particle, yet the myriad color scheme capability proves it is also a wave form.

Because, of this duality capability of light to be a particle and a wave form is demonstrated in the laser slit test, in much finer detail. The ability of light to be a particle and a wave simultaneously could be produce from the direct relationship or the "residual effect" that the singular monopolar slurry forms within the proximities reacting with other proximities.

Whereas, the proximity slurry is not a definite location at a definite time and not a single reactant. Read the above bold statement again, and quantify it in a quantum statement. In order to have closeness you have to have a single location in relationship to another location, and each location is separate from the other in all aspects except one…the fixed or stable location of one event to another event.

In the fixed physics world the closeness of proximities has to be fixed (even if it is a micro-nanosecond), in order to determine their effects not only upon themselves but, all fixed proximities around the particle.

The proximity slurry is always on the move, and if it stops, that atom—all that is physical, ceases to exist.

That is one reason or one effect that so called atom smashers have upon an atom…its proximity slurry is dramatically and traumatically altered. The monopolar adhesion is disrupted. However, because it is able to "regroup," itself or reestablish its monopolar adhesion is what prevents an unstoppable chain reaction from over whelming the universe. That effect was a great fear of Einstein and Oppenhimer.

Quantum Mechanics/Physics or the QMP requires the physical (the fixed laws) physicist to postulate that what if the random, or the "uncertainty of any given time and space," is not only a non specific predictable resonate or reactant but, a random resonate that affects its target with the proximity of resonate proximity randomness.

Could this resonate proximity randomness probability be equivalent to a monopolar slurry effect?

All objects as the underlining message in the movie The Incredible Shrinking Man all existence no matter how small or huge wants to occupy space, and therefore, give that space meaning and purpose. That meaning and purpose is postulated to be when space is no longer space and something occupies that space it has a purpose.

Thus the sub atomic particle that wants and theoretically needs to occupy all proximities gives or produces a purpose for the nuclei and the nucleus of the atom to stay active, to maintain its own identity, and keep its electron fog identity intact, and simultaneously allows the original identity of the electron fog to meld into a new identity, while maintaining a hidden original identity within the subatomic particle monopolar slurry.

The Math

As with most of the Feynman time and space graphs we conceptually accept time as on the left side going up and space or some disciplines "distance," as placed on the horizontal, going left from zero to infinity. The infinity from zero is for time as well.

I personally find it hard to accept zero time or zero space, as well as I do the concept of infinity in time or space. The reason I shun the zero to infinity concept is that no matter how small or how expanse, zero is always beneath or behind that point, and infinity is always pass that expansive point. To me going from zero to infinity we have no math…we have no true beginning nor no true end. However, as long as I stay just within zero and infinity I can see and work the math.

So, I call these range areas "positive zero" and "negative infinity" points.

The math is simple and yet complex to non abstract thinking. The CMET or the QMP slurry has no definitive right or wrong answers since the particles are always in motion passing through one proximity in relationship to all the other proximities.

The theorist in us all is show me. However, brilliant scientist such as Bohr, Rutherford, Heiensberg, Born, Schrodinger all contributed to the concepts of Quantum and Theoretical Physics. The Quantum Wave Theory that an electron cloud as they called it, is a statement or term for an electrons' path. However, that electrons' position is an uncertainty. As Planck's Constant states, "The Uncertainty in position times the Uncertainty of momentum is equal to what is called Planck's constant."

What does that formula state in terms of conditions or actions? Simply put, the more we try to identify an electrons' position we actually affect its position. Therefore, the fact or act of identifying an electron or in other words trying to identify it with a proton wave unit, or what we call light, interferes and slows down the electron. Thus making the position more uncertain and affecting the momentum. So Planck's Constant is a positional probability, and the thicker the cloud the more probability the electron maybe there.

The proton wave unit is a larger and therefore, has a more profound effect upon a particle's mass and velocity (several times more than the smaller mass size/effect, of the neutron). However, an electron with an electron energy level similar or less than the proton is proportionally affected and its momentum is altered by the effect of the proton wave unit acting upon it.

The electron cloud and the positional probability of uncertainties, as Planck put it is the very same counter punch qualifiers for the CMET fog and proximity slurry concept, as I will attempt to identify more.

Rutherford's coined the word "nucleus," and measured the size of atoms, for example Hydrogen nucleus maximum size was 3 X 10(-14) meters. This is very small compared to H atom size 1.0 X 10(-10) meters. As you can see the H atom is much larger. And inside the nucleus we have the protons, and the neutrons made up of the quarks. Quarks identified as Under, Down, Strange, Charm, Top and Bottom. The quarks are identified as Leptons as electron, Uon, Toall all negative (-) charged and the neutrinos Neutrino Electron (NE) , (N.Uon), and (N.Toall) all neutral charged.

The unique properties about Quarks and Leptons is that both behave as particles and/or waves. The "Particle Slit" test shows this dramatically, see drawing #1. The particle and wave action theory through a slit or series of slits reinforces each quark's and lepton's behavior. This is called the "Dual Nature of Particles."

Rutherford was concerned his theory would not hold totally true until Bohr supported his work by showing that electrons are in shells or orbits only and theoretically nothing existed in between these orbiting shells.

Bohr's math showed and proved that electrons could only occupy certain obits at certain times and at a certain electron energy level. Bohr discovered and calculated the radius of the rings or electron shells by using this formula. Please see the next few examples/drawings.

R= (5.2 X 10) X 1 (sq).   The one (1) squared is because we are talking about the first ring. Therefore, when talking about ring or orbit 2 the 2 is squared , the 3 square and the 4 squared until we get to "N" squared being an indefinite about of orbits.

By using these known constants Bohr also was able to calculate the speed by substituting known values.

V= $\frac{2.18 \text{ X } 10}{1}$ m/s Thusly, we have the distance of meters per second and it is divided by the shell number.

If we were talking about the # 4 ring we would divide by the # 4 m/s V= $\frac{2.18 \text{ X } 10}{4}$ m/s

By doing additional/ substitutions of known factors the electron energy potential can be calculated. This electron energy potential is called Electron Voltage (ev).

E= 13.6 – $\frac{13.6}{1}$ the 1 being the first ring or shell.

Thusly, the product would be 0.0 ev The 13.6 as being the constant factor. Therefore energy levels for the following....

Ring #1 = 0.0 ev   The rings are indefinite therefore, N or any number can be the divisor
Ring #2 = 10.2 ev
Ring #3 = 13.09 ev
Ring #4 = 12.75 ev

As stated Rutherford was concerned about his calculations and it was his assistant Bohr who actually proved his assumptions. Bohr calculations proved that each electron had an assigned orbit and that each electron would stay in that orbit until a free electron with more electron voltage differential equivalency intersected the electron in its orbit and transferred the differential potential with significant force to knock the electron out of its orbit into the next shell or ring.

By using the potential differentials we see how a free electron had to have exactly the same ev or more ev potential between the two shells to cause an electron to jump to the next ring, and that free electron absorbs any remainder ev .

Let's look at an example. The first ring we know has 0.0 ev and the free electron that strikes it has a 9.2 ev. Nothing happens except for an electron head butting and no jumping. The reason for no jumping is the free electron ev is not equal to or more that the difference between ring #1 (0.0ev), and ring #2 (10.2ev). However, there are bigger (more ev potential) electrons flying around and let's say this one is exactly 10.2 ev and slams into our #1 orbiting electron, and knocks it for a loop (dramatically speaking). It has enough potential difference to knock the #1 electron into the second ring. And the free electron receives the difference in this case no ev potential difference.   It may travel on or it may get caught up in the first ring since it has no ev potential.

If the potential difference of ev was more than 0.0 it would continue on its path. Since its remainder is more than 0.0 ev.

All these math statements presented by these famous individuals have earned their place in our history books many times over. It is with this same fever, not to be placed in any history file but, to find another fact about our universe, that present Celestial Monopolar Energy Transitions (CMET).

There are no real true secrets in our universe, only undiscovered facts that are not shared, yet.

Dr. Paul Diac's Observable Probabilities flavors the CMET slurry with its distinct melding of the three "mechanics" or physics. There are numerous math equivalent formulas of quantum mechanics/physics. Such as the one used is the transformation theory proposed by Cambridge theoretical physicist Paul Dirac, which combined and exemplified the foundations of quantum mechanics, matrix mechanics, and wave mechanics.

 In this assumption, the instantaneous state of a quantum system transcribes the probabilities of its measurable properties, or "observables". Examples of observables include energy, position, momentum, and angular momentum. Observables can be either be continuous (the position of a particle) or discrete (i.e. the energy of an electron bound to a hydrogen atom). Generally, quantum mechanics does not assign definite values to observables. Instead, it makes predictions using probability distributions; that is, the probability of obtaining possible outcomes from measuring an observable. Oftentimes these results are skewed or influenced by many variables or reactance's by many causes, such as dense probability clouds or quantum state nuclear attraction. Naturally, these probabilities will depend on the quantum state at the "instant" of the measurement. Therefore, uncertainty is involved in the value.

There are, however, certain states that are associated with a definite value of a particular observable event. These are known as "Eigenstates of the Observable." ("eigen" a German word for inherent). In the everyday world, it is natural and intuitive to think of everything (every observable event) as being in an inherent event.

Everything appears to have a definite position, a definite momentum, a definite energy, and a definite time of occurrence. However, quantum mechanics does not pinpoint the exact values of a particle for its position and momentum (since they are conjugate pairs) or its energy and time (since they too are conjugate pairs); rather, it only provides a range of probabilities of where that particle might be given its momentum and momentum probability.   The proximities to other proximities are inherent to the probability of the observable characteristics.

The eigen (or inherent probability) of an observable event is, that, if it is not here, then it must be there; or in other words its proximity to an observable event must be inherently related to a proximity to another observable event.

Maxwell's formula and others that are used to prove the magnetic fields are non monopolar and Delta magnetic fields equal (=) 0

In retrospect and respect for Einstein's famous theory E=MC^2 and out of my respect for the Great Creator CMET is technically born. Even though Einstein did not put "time" (T) in his famous equation it is definite implied because the speed of light squared is a time factor. Speed of light is as we know 186,000 mps that i time, and of course distance. Both of these are implied emphatically in the C^2 presentation.

Therefore, CMET is defined as follows:

C= speed of light and theological Celestial power which is the light of knowledge, or what all research seek define. However, it is also the definite containment of the nucleus Cell or its walls of containment.
M= mass as in Einstein's atomic mass and Magnetic momentum
E=energy (derived by E=MC^2)
T= speed-of-light/distance implied by Einstein and Transitions of proximities

CMET is found by taking the E=MC^2 formula and factoring in the transitions of proximities within a defin space (the atom's nucleus wall). The implied factor of Einstein's "time," based upon his distance covered i time (186,000 mps^2), and CMET time that the proximities take to transition through each proximity is the defining point for mono-polarity configurations.

Proximities within the nucleus cell wall does not have the "freedom," that Einstein's speed of light squared per se,' because, of the definite and defined containment of the nucleus cell itself.

In comparing the vastness and open space to let light waves travel and propagate (wave form) as they may without the containment walls that mono-polarity entities have to conform to, gives us a glimpse of the dissimilarities and at the same time the similarities of power or energy potential.

How do we define the power or energy potential of mono-polar singularities confined within the cell wall of atom's nucleus? That is actually, very simple once we define the energy within the nucleus of the atom by configuring Einstein's E=MC^2 formula. Let's look at element # 1...H= HYDROGEN.

I do not intent to "re-invent-the-wheel," so I am going to indicate my references so that all who have done th work can get the full credit of their work. I have enclosed a few pages of their hard work at the back of this brief mono-polarity supposition report.

As we can see the H atom has an E= to -13.26 divided by N2 (second shell or electron ring). This info was presented in several places within this report and how passing electrons have to have more energy potential dislodge an electron from its shell. Conversely the N#? will all have different energy levels, if the element h more than one energy/electron (Ev) ring (N), which H only has one (N1) Ev ring.

This Ev fog is caused by the speed of light/electron traveling around the atom. Thusly traveling also around nucleus of the atom to be exact. The negative charge of the electron into negative energy potential (-Ev) recognition is within itself a form of singular polarity, since all electrons are negative charged particles by th nature of their physics.

Putting this in a "wow factor," It is the ever so delicate balancing act of singular polarity electrons "dancing, within the close proximities of each other that maintain all states of matter, and it is their dissimilarities (Ev potential differences), that allow a single polarity electron into "bullying," the weaker electron into convertir into a different element. This is also what we call covalent compounding or elemental formulation...the act one atom giving up or receiving another electron to form a different element or molecule.

However, all that is within the "confines of space" (oxymoron). Whereas, the CMET is within the confines the nucleus cell wall, both with the same energy potential. Never-the-less the confines of space is a huge difference potential than the confines of a nucleus cell wall.

Spiritual Harmony Realm

The oxymoron "man-kind," has always been at odds or conflict with itself. More wars, torture, maiming, and death have been fought over the idea that someone's god is more powerful and their belief in their more perceived god is more important than others. Therefore, giving one the need and responsibility to prove that their god is better than anyone else's god....or should I say their professed belief in their god is more important than others profess belief's. Thus, this provides all the reasoning to have wars, and torture, and maim and kill those that do not believe the same way.

If I were a god, and some oxymoron did to others what some do, supposedly in its name, I'd be mad as hell!

And then we had those weirdoes like Buddha and Confucius who were always preaching or trying to teach that the path to enlightenment was to achieve harmony with one own inner being, or something like that. What we have all missed in these teachings is that not once did they say achieve natural harmony...they said *seeking the natural harmony was the pathway to peace and tranquility.*

So, what does the so called spiritual religious realm have to do with Mono-Polarity? Simple, if you just look at it logically...it is the seeking to be with all things within ourselves. It is that seeking or need to be at all places at once at all levels. It is this opposition to harmony and the attraction to achieve harmony that makes the pathway work. The mono-polarity of opposition to harmony and the mono-polarity of attraction seeking to be with itself in all places at once is the pathway, according to Confucius and Buddha....and maybe a few other weirdoes, too.

Has anyone ever really asked what happens when all things are in harmony....has anyone ever really logically looked at the possibility of what could happen if the what if of all things become harmonious? All entities have achieved a balance of opposition and attraction. There is no longer a need for or seeking for a balance, because all is balanced...

What If there is no need for opposition or attraction, because all is in perfect balance and harmony.

The simple logical answer is.... all that is in balance would cease to exist, because it has no need to exist. May be the word need is misleading? It has no individual opposition and attraction energy to exist. Supposedly, we can not create nor destroy energy. We can only alter it to perform different work. If there is no opposition or attraction, then energy can do no work.

Logically speaking then, all existences at all levels of time space and dimension must be individual entities? Or in other words....all entities must be Mono-polarities seeking to be in all places and all levels at once.

If we have no individual mono-polarities performing oppositions and attractions to be at all levels and all places at the same time, then we can not have any form of energy. And without energy we can have no work. And without any work we can have no life.

What if all existences was not made up of mono-polarities....what would be our existence then?

Spiritual and Scientific Mono-Polarity Logic

Bigoted arrogant self-proclaimed importance has always been at odds with each other as I stated. The only difference was usually if the self- proclaimed important arrogant bigot was behind the pulpit or the microscope. None of these oxymoron's took the time to logically ask what if there were no mono-polarities?

So much has been lost and never explored due to the oxymoron's too emotionally consumed to allow roo
logic.

I profess, I am no different than any of these oxymoron's either. I have no proof and I am not going to
chastise myself for not being able to "fabricate so-called proof. I could care less about the perceived
acceptance or rejection of proof of Mono-polarity. Some may feel that is very arrogant on my part...it is
arrogance at all it is logic.....

The logic of the acceptance or rejection of the logic of a mono-polarity universe is totally moot, as far as
logic is concerned...............................

A hundred trillion minds all saying the same thing does not make it so......nor does it disprove it.

What IF we had a Hundred trillion and one minds...would it make a difference?

I purposely left room for you to make WHAT IF notes???

****

What is UN-NEEDED STRESS due to Emotional Deprogramming

TEACHER and her kind are NOT without emotions because they choose to be, it is a lingering, gnawing at your gut feeling that is always in them as a result of the non-emotional DNA cross-breeding handed down from the Elders.

The LONGER the ET-BEING is away from the original DNA pure strain the more propensity for emotions manifest within the ET-BEING

So even like Spock they have to work at being non-emotional...and that is a real kick in the ass or head. Whichever body part you want to relate to. Personally, I have been told I am a "full figure female ass man."

Let's look at the cold HARD facts about a propensity to be "non-emotional." Notice I did NOT say the automatic ability to be non-emotional...but the propensity to be. There in again as Big Bill says, "Lies the rub."

The original humans that "converted" themselves to the first stage True Beings which were and are very similar to the True Being Elders did lose the ability to express emotions because, of the strength of the original batch of DNA used to convert the humans to what would be the original ET-BEINGS. However, as time and the actual separation from the pure TB bloodline and cloning the ET-BEINGS such as TEACHER and her kind are all having to "battle" the urge to express emotions.

I am not talking about how Spock had to be "stoic"...being stoic is not non-emotional. TEACHER and her kind all have the very crude ability to not only express emotions but to FEEL them as well. That super amount of suppression is damn stressful. That is one reason they do not live as long as they used to. Their average life span has been reduced down almost on average over a 110 years within the last 16 cloned generations. Their life span is 600-800+ years now.

Don't forget the Tue Being has to contend with 1,000s of star children, Phase 1 and Phase II inbreeds and conditioned humans on a 24/7 basis and they ALL are capable of expressing and feeling emotions and have no trouble or qualms about expressing the full energy of confusion, hurt, hate, love, ambivalence, and all those other million and one convoluted emotions the human mind can produce...actually it's probably closer to a billion maybe even a quadrillion 1 convoluted emotions instead of a mere million or so.

Image how hard it is for the True Being "Councilors" to keep their cool non-emotional self together having to contend with that crap day in day out 24/7...and without "hazard-duty-combat pay!"

Oh, you maybe asking why does TEACHER look like she does or why doesn't she look more "human" instead of a True Being? Simple answer is because "communicators" have to be the conduit between the interactive emotional target and the True Being and the Elders. TEACHER has to be as "pure" of heart and mind as a True being she can be and still communicate with the emotional rocks...such as myself.

****

As Aunt Jeremiah says...WEz allz diff-fer-entz!

Emotions that very thing we take absolutely for granted, and don't even try to say you don't because you know damn well you do...we ALL do, is the very thing we most learn from one way or another.

And I love it when people say stupid stuff, like "you MAKE" me so mad. horny, pissed, alone, scared, and a billion trillion other things we say people make us do, just like "the DEVIL made me do it!" Do you realize how absolutely bull-shit those blaming others for your feelings and resultant behaviors are? Since when does another person have the ability, power or "PERMISSION" to provoke another person to feel, behave, act or react?

Simple answer...NEVER unless we give them that power or permission to be responsible for our feelings, actions or reactions to any given situation. Realize it or NOT and admit it or not it is a hell of a lot easier blaming everyone else for your unwillingness to take responsibility for your own feelings action, reactions, perceptions and all that other hodgepodge of convoluted/twisted polluted stuff that makes us human and not like others...be those others from this world or not or even one human being from another.

"WEz allz diff-fer-entz!"

Not so true with the ET-BEINGS their family and hives are all basically the same as in it requires smaller crowbars and hammers to tweak out their differences.

IF Aunt Jeremiah statement is even half-way true...how can there be in legitimate realistic practical true science of "Psychology" that puts people's behavior in Pigeon holes as if it is "normal or not...Who is really to say what normal (according to the dictionary Normal is that which is repetitively done)...doing the same thing and expecting a different out-come is supposed to be crazy? Who or what is normal according to the dictionary may not be normal for another but who is to say it is "ABBY-Normal?"   Sort of kinda goes with that biblical statement...he who is without sin cast the first stone........I don't remember any rocks being thrown after that was said. Same logic goes for "censorship."   What censor does not have a bunch of skeletons in their closet? And the one I love almost most of all is "a trial by my peers".....where in hell are you going to find 6 or 12 weirdos who interpret life and rationalize about their perceptions like I do?

To say there are some "BLOW flies" in the rules is an understatement.

However, I realize we need an impression of rules just like we need the impression of freedom and pursuit of happiness and etc. Without those "perceptions" and NOT really having any viable feasible alternatives to those perceptions that is where in lies the rub again...no other viable feasible alternatives have been produced to provide a better recourse or the reality of "freely choosing" the lesser of two alternatives.

Again, no alternatives that TEACHER and her kind have and that and so much more was sacrificed when the first surviving humans sacrificed themselves for what they believed in heart, mind, body, and spirit was to give the human being a chance at survival if enough time could pass and that needed changes could be made so that man-kind in the future would not have to make those decisions and the ET-BEINGS of the future could be closer to that pure true advanced human that they are striving to be.

And since their future is not written that way they know that goal may never be achieved...and they accept that...and that is ONE reason they can NOT allow emotions to get in the way or over-shadow logic. The cold hard facts of logic...the logic of the mission out weights all else and everything and every being else, including the others and GREYS.

Who in this present day thinking would think the survival of man-kind was so paramount to the overall scheme of things and to those actors that have been in it, are in it, and will be in it?

And still to this very day...the present day human being with all their huffing and puffing pee in their pants at the slightest unknown, and still hide in the corner, even with all the lights turned on.

The closer we get to true Artificial Intelligence and Alternative Reality (AI/AR), to being a real reality the better I will feel about the goal I've jokingly set for myself the more optimistic I would feel about "my personal survival/continuation. However,

IF we were not so damn afraid of what we perceive as the FDA and the AMA and the big Phrams did not have such a strangle hold on the world's population I and all other humans would not have to worry about needing to become Androids or Cyborgs in order to survive because our ET-BEING breather would be sharing with us the super advanced technologies that would kick organized religions butt to make present day man kinds' virtually disease and illness free. Which you can damn well bet organized religion and those three letter agencies do not want to lose all that profit fat catting money making control they have on you and me...presently.

Do you understand the power/impact that above paragraph has to us present day human beings? The "few" that actually manipulate the worlds control to what does and does not transpire in the earth populace. That also includes the military corporations that Eisenhower specifically talked about in his public speech. Think about what he did not say but meant...if we did not have wars or the threats of war what need would there be for the banking cartels to fund these billions of dollars that could be used to the productive benefit of the man-kind populace.

What IF there <u>never was a need</u> for the ET-BEINGS to exist to save our sorry asses?

"Oh, Happy days are here again...before he walked"... man-kind walked on the face of the earth.......... Somewhere!

```
******************************************************************
```

TEACHER, ESP, TELEPATHIC, TELEKINESIS TRANSPORTATION Brain/ Light Waves, Frequencies and...

Getting any ideas yet? I am not telling you to do this, but reading all the other ET-BEINGS books will give you a lot of incite into this area, and a lot more and should prepare you better for the classes you may choose to take or to purchase and understand the DVDs better/easier.

Hey! You ask...why so short of a segment? Good question. As soon as you have a good answer be sure to let us know? I'll give you a hint...it probably would take another book to explain, and I may not feel like doing it, too....remember a LOT was shared that I have not shared, or I may not intend to share either. There was no rule that said I had to share everything that was shared with me, my spiritual bloodline over the eons....Next time you have a few extra 1,000 years or so to spare, I might try to bring you "into the ballpark" of what has been shared with me and my spiritual bloodline. Don't forget there are a LOT more OTHERS out there that not only "interact" with this earth/time line etc....But with a Lot more in our cosmos....the true GREYS, and others in addition to TEACHER and her kind and all the modifications of ET-BEINGS it is getting to be so convoluted you can't tell them apart unless they have a name tag...and those damn shape shifters are really sneaky about their "true identity." See why I say it is another book just by itself?

```
******************************************************************
```

"M" as in "Moving-On"...CONDITION HUMANS'

This area I did not go into a lot of detail and sort of just left everything "hanging" as to hun?

Well, I will attempt to provide a little more clarification here as to why a generalized present day human being would "freely" choose to live among other conditioned humans, Tue Beings, and Phase 1 and Phase 2 Inbreeds (star children). There are also the new breeds of Indigos, Auroras and a few newly developed off-springs that are being "grown" and/or cloned with certain gene modifications to accomplish the overall mission requirements.

To answer the question based upon many conversations that I have had and still do with condition humans, I hear basically the same answer over and over again. What would be the prevailing predominate reason that these men and women choose freely (remember TB read their thoughts), to make this decision? It is actually very simple once you hear it being said time after time in words that are all very similar from these 1,000s of conditioned humans.

Relationships, Commitments, Responsibilities etc.

Reader WARNING: Some of this information may be too intense for kiddies and Prudes!

Ask yourself do you fall into any other three areas mentioned above? Are you in a relationship? Is that relationship making you feel inside that you are in over your head? It does not matter if you are married or not, or how long you have been in this relationship...does it "full-filled you" or does it make you feel lost, confused, lonely abused, neglected, empty or a 1,001 other "bad feelings?"

Do you care enough for this person and yourself not to intentionally hurt this person by just leaving and they be able to "Blame You," for leaving them? Would having them be able to blame you and rightfully so be unbearable...more unbearable than staying in the relationship that makes your insides feel so crappy all time...making you mentally and yes, Physically sick. Are you openly or secretly hoping for a quick death to get out of feeing so terrible?

How many 100s of thousands of you out there right now can say yes to most of these questions? There are millions!

How many of you feel over-whelmed with commitments to others? The loved one who needs constant care and you are totally 100 % unable to do a damn thing to make their suffering any better. Do you feel guilty when you wish they would just die, so they did not have to suffer anymore. Aren't you really saying I'll be glad when you die so "I" will not have to see you suffer anymore and I can get on with my life and do what I can to contend to being without you, and not feel guilty, helpless, and totally inadequate any-more.

How many have gotten in over their heads in debt, buying a house or some other major purchases, or have a gambling addiction and drugs, sex or a 1,001 addictions that make accepting responsibility so immeasurable difficult to do and accept?

What do all three of these categories and ET-BEINGS have in common?

Simple...No ONE has to be responsible or feel guilty, or like they let everyone down if they made the decision to leave. However, IF the ET-BEING can be realistically blamed for taking their husband, wife, brother or sister away then there is virtually no more guilt of freely leaving.

The one left behind per se' that was causing all the negative feelings now has someone/something to blame and not the person who left.

Sure at first there are the normal guilt feelings that the conditioned human feels about freely leaving and choosing to live on a star ship with 1,000s of others of their kind and millions of those that are not "human" per se.' But that is what is called conditioning.

Every disease, discomfort and negative physical, mental trait of the human that is flawed is fixed one way or another by the True Beings advanced medical, electronic, and energy technology.

For example the mental conditional programming of the male in regards to "porn" is nothing like the tamed G rated XXX stuff we have now that all the "church bitties" are all up in arms about. Virtual Reality and Alternative Reality that the ET-BEING has for training and conditioning the male is so much more advanced than what we have now. Every sensation, stimuli perception, reception and reaction is so much more physical and mental stimulated.

There is definitely no Erectile Dysfunction with a condition male. After all most ED is 85% in the head (brain), and the organic ED is fixed and cleared up to be just like the male was 19 years old again and never ages in the "Erector set department."

The male is not only free but encouraged to visualize whatever fantasy he chooses and he can feel physical emotionally mentally and even spiritually every little sensation that he chooses and even to what extent he chooses...i.e. for how long

The sexual performance area is just one part that is conditioned and the males' physical and mental physic image is enhanced as well. Plus the male or female Never has to worry about coming into contact with the person that they were in the relationship with because those brain wave patterns are tracked and monitored 24/7...there Never has been a close encounter with the wrong person when involving the conditioned human...male or female.

Speaking of males and females, there are no "true" homosexuals in the Conditioned Human areas. The human can be a bi-sexual however, their sexual "performance" has to be just as active/intense of the opposite sex interactive partner. However, the human's fantasies AI/VR episodes do not have any restrictions on any sexual excursions. It can be as homo sexual pedophile as it can be imagined. These safe fantasy "exercise" areas are segregated and totally isolated from the "public" areas, and the conditioned human can be as active, loud, and active as they choose in a safe protective area. The totally sound proof area is really preferred by the women especially those women who have multiple orgasms in one session.

Prudes and kiddies warning: As I stated the advancements in VR/AR are "powerful" compared to the 21st century man-kind of "porn/sexual fantasy escapisms...for example:

The male penis is encased in a masturbator that is so tactical functioning that it can very effectively be an oral sexual unit and then with the thought turn into a female vagina that is wet and "muscular grabs the penis." The oral sex and/or the fornication action can last past the time the male ejaculates and sexual partner definitely can swallow and not spit it out. The waves of ejaculated climaxing is maintained as long as the participant chooses and the ejaculate is NOT wasted. The ejaculate is sucked out as the fantasy continues and collected. This ejaculate is analyzed for sperm count, viability, strength, and most important the improving the survivability of the DNA in the human as far as man-kind survivability mission is concerned. If the male can perform to ejaculate more than once then so much more the pleasure and the ejaculate analysis that takes place.

Also what needs to be explained is the interaction of the conditioned human and earth female that is designed to impregnating the earth female. This bloodline interaction/encounter that produces a child that will invariability be encountered/abducted multiple times in its life times. This earth/conditioned human off-spring that results from the sexual encounter with the earth female and the conditioned human male may be offered the option to become a conditioned human as well during its life time. Also there may be only one encounter, and the medical testing results be "ordinary/unacceptable" as a need to encounter/abduct just once. It all depends upon what these very important medical exams reveal presently and what hypnotists of future needs in regards to the mission's requirements.

The conditioned female is built and physically reconditioned from head to toe. She is provided with the right amount of full bust and hips that are firm and rounded and not saggy. Neither she nor the male are maintained at their age. In other words the male is "re-made" to be around the very early 20s (sexual performing peek years), while the female is made no older than 27 but, most are remade to be 24 years of age (optimum sexual reproductive years), body, mind, emotions and spiritually wise.

Again she can not be mentally a true homosexual, and can be a bi-sexual or heterosexual is preferred. She has the most super advanced sexual AI/VR/AR technologies offered to her... a lot more options than the male for "more/ intense" sexual fantasies especially, since she can and is highly encouraged to achieve multiple orgasms in one session.

She is in this sound proof room where she can moan and verbally exclaim her enjoyment as loud/intense as she feels free to do while she is lying or reclining in her special designed chair.

She is free to interact physically with her hands as she chooses or the special chair has the ability to perform all the physical tactile actions that she desires from head to toe. She can have her head/hair mussed while her breast are massaged and the nipples can be sucked and "tongue rolled", and have the air vacillate between hot breath and cool sucking on the nipple(s).

Her tummy down to the clitoris and if chosen the ass rectum can all be stimulated to any extent that she chooses, and as deep as she chooses. And she is not limited to a human partner for her fantasy...she is open to any fornication machine she chooses with as many of "extensions (dildos), and in any configuration that she chooses. There is no limit to the vibrators and internal/external "toys" as she chooses and just like the male there are no limits to the number and type of partners. If she likes "well hung" little boys who are very talented she is free to fantasize that to her heart and orgasm(s) content.

She knows she is monitored to her body's reactions that is actually monitored through her sex partner chair and as with the male the brain waves are monitored as they are automatically transmitted. The monitoring is as autonomous as much as possible to not "taint" or skew any of the monitoring results.

As stated before, the eyesight, hair skin imperfections and any other negative attribute is erased and/or fixed on the volunteering conditioned human. And naturally because of all these improvements and health programs the conditioned human lives a lot longer than common stressed to the max earth humans do now.

It is not uncommon to talk with conditioned humans that are 250--400 years young and still going strong. So the number of sexual encounters and reproductions/birthing's is not as near "stressful as you thought, because it is NOT in our normal life span time span but in their highly advanced time span.

She has a very vital role in being the carrier of reproductively not only with interactive encounters with earth humans but with other conditioned humans and she has the free choice to sexually interact with Phase 1, Indigos, and those that are sexually endowed. Naturally there is NO True Being sexual contact as there are no sexual organs on True ET-BEINGS'.

The birthing she provides in her womb or in the bovine is monitored closely and the DNA that the offspring is measured and evaluated as to purpose use and bloodline strength.

Realistically the conditioned human play a very significant role in helping the ET-BEING achieve the mission ultimate goal. And that one reason is programmed into the conditioning to reduce the human emotion of guilt as to understanding and acceptance in a more peaceful being.

The conditioned man and woman is what the ET-BEING is striving to be...only in a more advanced mental, emotional, physical and spiritual state.

And NO, just because you may like what you read hear does NOT mean you can volunteer to be a conditioned human...there is no application form. Only after a specific encounter, testing are you offered the opportunity to become a conditioned human. The ET-BEINGS' AI computer chooses you according to your bloodline and Their need of what May be in your specific DNA....sorry

WHAT IF no one freely chose to be a conditioned human? Where would mankind's survival rating be at...instead of where it is now???

****

"T" AS IN TRANSPLANTEE

This was not a total successful experiment that had generations of planning and decades of testing to determine its productivity to the mission's main requirement. The fact as stated in **ET-BEINGS 1 A Report On Extraterrestrial Communications** that the transplantee's physical body gave out a lot sooner on average than the normal life span of a non-transplantee human was very dishearten to the True Beings who put a lot of time and detailed study into the technology required to transplant a modified ET-BEINGS spirit into an earth fetus before the "official" spirit was in it was very difficult to do and "stage."

The Roswell staged UFO crash probably had one of the last transplantee events to take place. There were a few others before Roswell but these were in very secluded areas and the ET-BEINGS had nothing to do with what happened. I will say it, and the transplantee event was not a UFO crash it was another event that happened near Taiwan on 02/28/1947. One of those protesters so badly burned charcoal bodies was a Phase 1 ET-BEING that had his spirit transplanted into an earth child almost 8,000 miles away (as the crow flies). This earth child was scheduled to receive his earth spirit within a few hours of the transplantee trans-positioning. The Phase 1 ET-BEING allowed himself to be set ablaze to disguise his appearance. To the world he was just another burned protester in a group of over 30,000 dead protestors. But everything had to be timed down to the very minute nanosecond (time differences etc.), because this fetus as stated was a few weeks old and ready for the human spirit to take charge of his development.

I realize I never really did go into what a transplantee really is and what all it entails. I did elude to it and I also eluded that as I understood from TEACHER I was a transplantee. However, I think it was my ego that made me think I was from a staged Roswell crash. If I was going to a transplantee I heard what I wanted to hear and Roswell being what it is and actually what it means to me...well one assumption lead to another, and we both know what that makes me. I will claim in my defense that I was going to move there when I was younger and I had a teaching job at the ROTC already lined up but, as things happen it did not happen as I planned.

As far as I know the two transplantees from Roswell have not made themselves known, yet. As I said, they "burn-out" faster and they both may be dead by now?

This was supposedly the time when TEACHER and I "retired." However, we all know better, I and TEACHER never really retired...we just got better at communicating at a different (higher), level than when I was stressing out about "life's events." I had to learn what the famous "philly-sopicer ZIGGY" preached..."Don't take life so damn serious...the shortest distance to true understanding and acceptance in knowing that you can't do a damn thing about IT... lies between our two ears.

The fetus as discussed briefly in other ET-BEINGS books is at first just a hunk of jellied plasmatic stuff doing its dividing as in multiplying its number of cells into "something." But contrary to all the religious dogma it is not with a life spirit yet. The process is a preprogrammed routine to produce something from the union of an egg and a fertilizing cell into now a fertilized egg. The mitosis and all those other tosis are not a viable product, yet but in a few weeks it will be...it will have gained its life spirit. That is when it is a Living being. I hate to say this but a lot of abortions are taking living beings and breaking them viciously apart in a very inhumane vacuum cleaner.

Transplantees are ET-BEINGS who for the sake of the mission volunteer to sacrifice themselves (actually their spirit), to activate a human fetus before the human spirit takes over. The technology for this to take place is truly remarkable and it is down to the finest tuning of brain wave co-habitation that allows this to take place.

The fetus has to have a functioning brain to produce the acceptive brain wave co-habitation and there can be no human spirit residing within the fetus as of the time the transplant takes place.

That means if the brain is just the slightest slow in developing acceptable cohabitive brain wave functions the spirit could take over before the targeted child is ready and the ET-BEING sacrificed its being for nothing. The spirit of the ET-BEING can only survive 9 Earth minutes MAX before it is gone, and not viable for transplanting.

Why only 9 minutes? Because the energy that is needed to maintain the brain wave after it leaves the host is only capable of storing enough energy to keep the brain wave viable for 9 earth minutes maximum. It actually starts to deteriorate after four minutes and the energy is depleted totally around 8 minutes and 35—59 seconds. Actually, if the ET-BEING's spirit is away from the host after 6 minutes the transplant mission is scrubbed.

Another problem is that if the targeted fetus is NOT a product of a union between a conditioned human and an earth woman the process is more difficult because of the internal DNA coding favorably preferring a human spirit instead of an ET-BEINGS transplantee spirit. The DNA from the conditioned human impregnating the female provides a more accessible acceptance for the ET-BEING transplantee spirit that would not be there other-wise.

Once the fetus accepts the ET-BEINGS spirit then everything as far as the human is concerned is "speeded-up." Like I said, a 9 volt DC motor being constantly fed by a 12 Volt DC battery. See **ET-BEINGS 1 A Report On Extraterrestrial Communications** for additional info and incite into how this makes a person feel on the inside, practically since day one.

****

A" AS IN ADAPTIVELY AND ACCEPTANCE OF ABDUCTIONS

This may be one of the most important chapters that I write or teach about, and I want to do it the very best I can. So, please bear with me and give me some slack as I try to explain these very personal and often very traumatic events to where you may allow yourself to feel better.

I am using the word abduction here because that is actually what it is as far as you are concerned. The ET-BEING sees and understands it different because of the severity of the mission requirement.

That is to ensure that man-kind as a species survives at all cost above all other needs.

That mission statement even grossly out weights the desire NOT NEED but desire of the ET-BEING not to be who they are in order for man-kind to survive.

From day one that the few surviving humans who made the ultimate sacrifice to become the ET-BEING that comes back in time to try to save man-kind... that has always been the mission and the ONLY mission. Despite everything we present day man-kind do now to deny, cover up and destroy any and all records or possibilities of the ET-BEINGS in our world.

They knew we would be doing all these things and more...even removing our own fellow humans who stood in the way of the massive denial cover-ups that had to take place in order for those in control to maintain that control.

I am not going to spell it out for you...if you want to know more, then do your own research, and formulate your own opinions. I think you might be shocked by what you find and definitely don't find.

The only way you are going to feel any internal piece about what you "think" you experienced or did not experience is to educate yourself where you are alone as much as possible with your own thoughts to rationalized your perceptions of events, times, places etc.

I am not going to tell you that it was not frightening, because your memories and perceptions tell you different...that it was "horrifying as far as you are concerned.

All I ask is please do your own research and analyze for yourself. Even if your read all my books and attend my classes and/or buy my DVDs (soon to be made), there are other educated experts who has incites and bits and pieces here and there. However, take everything you read (including my stuff), with an open challenging mind to where you feel comfortable with your decision. It does not matter if the rest of the world feels it is right wrong or a bunch BS or the next best thing to whole wheat bread (better for you than white bread)...it all matters down to what it means to you and How it truely/freely allows you to feel.

Defensive Symbiotic Impregnations...no you are not made pregnant by them...they are the non-removable (hypnosis), defensive memories that are actual cells placed near the gut (second brain—**ET BEINGS 2 A TEXTBOOK UPDATED),** that motivates you to feel the way you do about your encounter/abduction.

Because this is personal I have made an open invite on my web site www.etbeings.com to contact me about your feelings of being abducted, encountered. Visited, interacted with...whatever, you call it and I will try to provide some reasoning to your event. Remember, there are those that are troubled by the events and there are those that want to have more to learn and share more. Neither or any concerns one way or another will be judged. If you have read my books I think you will understand that a lot better, as I talk about each of these perspectives in every book and class.

****

FACE READING and OTHER UNIQUENESS'S of THE EXTRATERRESTRIAL 101

WOW! How to read the faces of an ET-BEINGS'?   That has to be one of the most outlandish ideas anyone could come up with to write about. But it is actually true as far as being able to read an ET-BEINGS' facial features and determining "sort of" what "personality" this ET-BEING is prone to be like…if it could express emotions; and in there again lies the rub as Big Bill says.

I also plan on touching or introducing other areas of man-kinds transitions with our ET—Ancestors as they have performed "tangents" in the human spirits existence and then followed the prime directive of not interfere with our chosen destiny. However….

That part about not interfering as in the Star Trek Prime Directory is NOT totally true or applicable…there seems to be a GREY matter in the "ruling."

Ever wonder when we talk about our "little gray cells as Hercule Poirot says, that we may be talking about "LITTLE GREY CELLS and their influences/interferences.

If you have read my other books on ET-BEINGS you should know by now or assumed/presumed (depending if you want to be the "ass' (as in **ass**uming). or a calculating risk taker), of understanding my "histories" with ET-BEINGS, and especially my relationship with TEACHER.

I plan on developing this book by showing either photographs and/or drawings of humans (homo-sapiens) that are in what we call the "present-today man." This is no pun or misstatement against women as

I plan to use comparisons of human females and males as much as possible. These human comparisons will then be identified in the "face of the ET-BEING" as much as possible. However, the features of the ET-BEINGS' face will be less pronounced or evident as on the human face.

This book: **ET-BEINGS 4** section on "Face Reading of the Extraterrestrial,"   could provide significant incite into uniqueness's of the ET-Being. Over my decades of my interactions with TEACHER and other of and not of her kind I have noticed certain characteristics are "relatable" to the entities facial features or lack thereof as well.   Just like human's facial feature are "readable" so are extraterrestrials…to a certain extent.

Science of face and body reading is a well-known and recognized science of correlating certain similarities to certain behavior patterns. I grant you that is going to be more abstract when we are discussing basically non-emotional entities, such as TEACHER and her "family" but not her hive (relatable Phase 1/II inbreeds, Star Children, conditioned humans and others not affiliated with TEACHER), at all.

I can see from the very beginning of formulating this idea that the book would require numerous drawings to depict the subtitles of what I'd be making the comparisons of human species behavior, and that of the target extraterrestrial beings.

I will strive to indicate the exact subtlety of the ET-BEINGS' features as it relates to the proven science of reading faces.

Also in reading faces the oriental face is distinctly different than a European face as is their DNA chain. The oriental face is actually somewhat "easier" to correlate or make a comparison to the ET-BEINGS' features of certain ET-BEING families and hives. If you have read my other books you will understand why I say that in relationship to blood lines and other DNA mixing and histories that the ET-BEING has with the human being in our futures.

True ET-BEINGS have or demonstrate no "personalities" per se.' So, how do you read or presume a trait not only in the face but other unique traits within and presented (façade), an ET-BEING that would be similar in a human being?

Good question…that type of question is what makes this such a unique book☺!

Well, let's look at a well-known presumption of face reading:

EYES:

The human who has a wide bridge nose that separates the eye's width making the distance between the eye's ratio in relationship to many other factors of the skull/face are often seen as "wide-thinkers." The same is true with the "classic" ET-BEINGS' face. Even though they have a very narrow nose area the minute different distances between the classic big black eyes and also for all hybrids (which I will cover in a lot more detail later on in the book), are seen by other ET-BEING unit as "stable decision makers" for the good of the family/hive. Individual hybrid in-breeds are seen as very cautious before acting on an emotional action/reaction/stimuli.

Getting past your fears and inherent survival instincts are going to be only way to really study the face of the ET-BEING, and yes, the ET-BEINGS must allow you to have full unrestricted observable and cognitive reasoning access to the ET-BEING and to yourself as well. This may require several direct interactions (abductions as you call them), that progress in acceptance of each other's presence.

You, must be totally honest with yourself, and the ET-BEING within these interactions, why...don't forget that they are a lot better at reading your mind than you are at reading and understanding theirs.

As I was saying let's look at the eyes...even for ET-BEINGS they are "windows to the soul." I hope I have established well enough that the ET-BEINGS as one are technically more reverent to the all-powerful spirit than man-kind is because of our ego motivation spiritual requirements.

In the following example we see a face of a present day human being; and the face of a presumed present day ET-BEING (based upon so many visitation documented accounts etc.).

Before I write anything else about what "science" says, why don't you just look at the human and conjecture an idea what this human being is like. Make some quick short notes if you want just to confirm your "impressions" before reading what "science" says. Now, do the same for the ET-BEING...what would this entity be like if it could freely express emotions?

And don't forget all most all the different ET-BEINGS species want to be able to be advanced as they are and be able to express emotions, freely.

Just like when we see humans we see the eye's first and then depending we scope out the rest of the face and body. However, the fear factor for most by now has "over-loaded," our reasoning circuits, and we have undoubtedly sweated a lot and/or peed more than a "laugh trickle/tinkle."

Non-Emotional Response Propensity

I know you, the reader is asking that question or something very similar in content or context. If a being is non-emotional responsive how am I going to identify any behavior traits? Simple answer…you're not.

This "face-reading" of the ET-BEING is presented to you so you can see or observe the subtle differences in the ET-BEING and others from what I will call the "safety of your arm-chair or couch."

These distinctions are presented as "if you were there" and you were not scared and just having a normal ole' everyday telepathic conversation with a being who you have learned how to be open-minded, yourself, comfortable to broadcast your thoughts openly without reprisals as I have over the decades as I have been associated with TEACHER and others of her kind, in addition to Phase 1//2 inbreeds (Star/Aurora-children), Indigos, and conditioned humans and others.

You would see the distinct differences in their faces and other physical traits that do produce emotional restraints or actual behavior actions.

Remember, only the True Being (direct decedents from the Elders), is void of all emotions………all others are a form of controlled or modulated emotional reaction control…including the conditioned human.

I'll use TEACHER's face and an Elder for comparison in the next few drawings

This is a close rendering of Elders face.

This is a very accurate drawing of TEACHER. Do you see the subtle differences from TEACHER's face and the ELDER?

1). Did you see TEACHER's face is wider and more fuller than an ELDER with overall softer lines in its construction even in chin/jaw area.

2). Do you see the eyes are slightly larger and cleaner (more reflective) of the area she is viewing,

3). Do you see the actual eyelid over the top of the eye (no lashes)

4). Do you see the eyes are actually set a very slight distance inward (deeper into the skull) than in the Elder?

5). Do you see her skin around the eyes, nose and especially the forehead are cleaner and "younger" looking (she is younger than the Elder)?

6). Do you see she has fuller lips (her modification for communication—if needed), than the Elder? It is full enough to appear she has a slight "lip liner."

7). Look at the forehead area…the skin is tighter and has less modulating vertical ridges than the Elder.

8). Did you see how the nostril's of the nose of Teacher is more rounder and softer than the more angular nostril's of the Elder? However, also notice that the Elder nose/bridge/nostril area are more defined than those of other extraterrestrial beings have a "sharp-cut-off" type nose with very narrow slits for nostrils and these beings are not of the same family/hive of TEACHER and her kind.

9). Elders lips are very narrow and less advanced formed than TEACHER's modified cloned sculpted lips are. Even though the Elders lips are less defined they are still more observable/functioning than those of other extraterrestrials whose mouth is very narrow, short and only opens enough to consume the food…a thick highly nutritious paste.

10). Not shown but discussed in brief detail in previous books the food as a vibrant paste makes the need for a shorter gut/digestive track and going to the bathroom to eliminate body waste a lot more efficient for all species of the extraterrestrials. I grant you that is very difficult to determine just by looking at their faces:-)

11). There are other areas that are evident but only when you look close…like ears, chins jaw line etc.

So how does this compare to the human behavior as far as "Face Reading" is concerned…what hidden behaviors lurk in the science of reading the human face?

As I said earlier, computers normally track our eyes to see what we look at first when we see a person…we also do this when we see the ET-BEING as well.

Why are the ET-BEINGS eyes the way they are? A very good question that I did not go into a lot of detail before. I will do what I can to explain why and how the ET-BEINGS eyes' are the way or constructed the way there are and how gene construction was developed.

The Chinese Mantis DNA was chosen due to its behavior to usually be very docile and quiet. It does not travel far if its food source is close or near by and readily available however, It will stalk a prey especially if it is kept in a cage as a pet as many Asians do. Even if it is not normally aggressive it will strike a protective/defiance pose when threatened.

The Eyes: Praying Mantis (Chinese Mantis- *Tenodera sinensis)*,

  Do the eyes look familiar? This is NOT a rare photo of the Mantis' eyes…there 1,000s that show the black eye covering. What is not basically known about the Mantis eye is that it is 5 lenses in one. The True Beings had to modify the 5 down to the 3 stereoscopic 6

dimensional viewing plane that most (not all) Terrestrial ET-BEINGS have now.

Below is a rough drawing of the Mantis 5 lens eye and how it is a simple 5 lens system that is covered by a domed lens that projects a very dark background, very similar to the photo above and 1,000s that you will see all over the Internet.

The blackening of the lens serves several functions from protection to projecting a cleaner image against a high contrast background. This visual configuration is vital to the safety of the Mantis and especially to the ET-BEING is its everyday life and space travels.

If you feel compelled to do more research on the Mantis especially why the Cyborgs chose the DNA from the Chinese Mantis then feel free…the Internet has a vast reference library on the Mantis and its unique qualities that the original True Beings and the Cyborgs "desired" or NEEDED to construct the ancestral ET-BEING as the cyborgs summarized would be needed for the humans to survive.

However, it was in the beginning all a crap shoot a go for broke risk!

EYES ARE SAID TO BE WINDOWS TO THE SOUL

Reader, please note that some of these drawings are not as well done as I would have liked. I had to do some "on the run," if you get my drift especially, when I was being "associated with" the OTHERS or as some call Reptilians Draconian or GREYs. They are NOT GREYs.

The Reptilian species is more "vigorous" in their encounters with humans or any other "sub-species, and this is even true with their exchanges with TEACHER and her kind. True the Reptilian is older, but being older does not make you more better, or "humane loosely speaking" nor more wisdom balanced to go with the advanced technology. Most of the Reptilian tribes are just that way.

And when it comes to an Ass kicking contest by a bully the Others will inadvertently always beat the terrestrial beings' ass (human and ET-BEINGS). So yes, some of these drawings are hurriedly done.

What does the Mantis 5 eyes look like in relationship to the ET-BEINGS three… 6 dimensional eyes. You may need to refer to the other books especially **ET-BEINGS 2 A TEXTBOOK UPDATED**...there are a few very descriptive drawings in it and actually explains the eyes from **ET-BEINGS 1 A REPORT ON EXTRATERRESTRIAL COMMUNICATIONS** a little better.

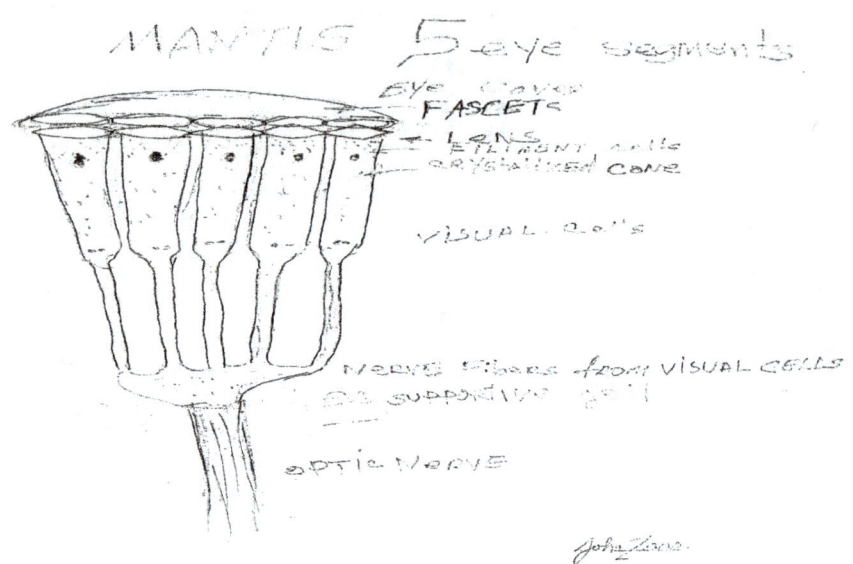

Below are common human eye shapes (without brows or lashes)

EYE ANGLES

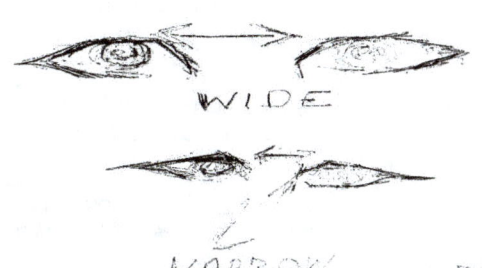

WIDE

NARROW
Closely spaced

DOWARD Slope
ANGLE

EYE ANGLES cont.

FLAT—no angle

UPWARD Slope ANGLE

Face Reading according to the recognized science of face reading (very similar in acceptance as Astrology, Numerology and Body Language).

EYES we usually see the eyes first of a human and of a space alien. What do the eyes tell us in a very brief explanation. You looked at the eyes drawn what were your conclusions in relationship to the "experts?"

Wide Eyes (as wide if not wider than the eye—see arrow showing width). *"NORMALLY SEEN AS A BROAD MINDED THINKER WHO SEES THE BIG PICTURE AND DOES NT LIKE GETTING LOADED DOWN WITH DETAILS. THOSE WITH NARROW EYES OFTEN CONSIDER THE WIDE EYED PERSON AS AN "AIR-HEAD" FREE THINKING UNREALISTIC OPTIMIST. MONEY OFTEN ELUDES YOU BECAUSE YOU OFTEN FAIL TO SEE THE REALIST MONETARY GAINS FOR YOUR EFFORTS.*

The following are my "observations" there is NO "proof" from what I am writing, just an opinion...some people who are star sign/ascendant of Gemini who are "writers" are very visionary, but do not get the recognition they desire because they fail to allow the little details of their writings show through. Take time to see each petal of the rose and how it is constructed and you will be a better writer...I can not say you will get the fame you want, though. Handwriting is often flowery and fat, slow, and thick.

Narrow eyes (seen as "wide" slits and close together). *OFTEN SEEN AS VERY EXACTING AND FOCUSED ON DETAILS . JOBS THAT REQUIRE EXTREME ATTENTION LIKE ACCOUNTING, RESEARCH AND LAW ENFORCEMENT ARE USUALLY CHOSEN BY PEOPLE WITH NARROW EYES. THEY HAVE A HARD TIME SEEING THE GRAY IN A B/W WORLD.*

Opinion: If you are a Virgo or ascendant is Virgo or Sagittarius often these people are so ridged they have a high propensity to be OCD and/or problems with parents/authority figures. If the sun rises in Scorpio often this person could be very stubborn and hard-headed and can not be convinced else wise, even if the facts disagree with their strict way of seeing things. Handwriting is often sharp and thin and digs into the paper.

Sloped Downward (the outer corner slants downward): *DOWNWARD SLANTED AT THE CORNER EYES OFTEN PRESENTS A PERSON WHO IS NOT A HIGHLY MOTIVATED OPTIMIST. AS A "REALIST" PEOPLE OFTEN TALK WITH YOU ABOUT THEIR PERSONAL PROBLEMS. THIS MAKES YOU A NATURAL COMMUNICATOR, COUNSELOR, AND CLERGY. HOWEVER, THE NEGATIVE PROFILE CAN CLOUD YOUR JUDGEMENT AS TO BE NON-FORGIVING (OPPOSITE OF CLERGY "TEACHINGS")..THESE ARE OFTEN NUNS WHO RAPP YOU KNUCKLES.*

Opinion: Those who are Capricorns or Leo rising demand traditional loyalty especially in family routines...this is even stronger in Scorpios. These sun and physical profiles can be controlling and make very strict bosses with no excuses attitude. As military leaders there is no deviation from regulations. Hand writing is sharp but readable and applied into the paper with alternating pressures.

FLAT NO ANGLE (EYE LID IS FLAT ACROSS TOP): *OFTEN SEEN AS A "REALIST OPTIMIST" IN OTHER WORDS YOU TRY TO SEE BOTH TOP/BOTTOM OF THE GLASS IS FULL OR NOT. YOU OFTEN WEIGHT THINGS BACK/FORTH TO ACHIEVE A PERCEIVED BALANCE. OFTEN HAVE LOTS OF FRIENDS AND SEEN AS A "DECENT PERSON."*

Opinion: If LIBRA is your Ascendant then you are seen as humorous, nice caring and nurturing of others. You usually have dimples in your cheeks (both face and butt). You try to see the good and the harmonic bad in everything as you strive for balance. In extremes it can be difficult to make a decision by taking too long to decide. Writing is often clean, clear and well-formed letters because understanding is important to you as you are a natural teacher.

UPPER SLOPED (SOMETIMES SEEN AS CAT-EYES): *OFTEN "POLLYANNA'S" HAVE THESE EYES AS THEY TRY TO SEE THE BEST IN EVERYTHING AND EVERYONE. THIS CAN BE TROUBLESOME FOR SOME AS BEING TOO TRUSTING ESPECIALLY THOSE THAT CONTROL AND/OR ABUSE. THESE UPPER SLOPED EYES KEEP THINKING THE "BAD WILL GET BETTER." OFTEN THESE PEOPLE ARE ATTRACTIVE (ESPECIALLY FEMALES), AND THIS CAN SET THEM UP TO BE HURT EASY AS THEY LOVE QUICK AND HARD.*

Opinion: If your sun/star sign are any of the "humanitarian signs" things do not always get better just because you want them to. Your open friendly nature is often in support of others and that can be a real rewarding karma positive energy event. However, if that trust is "BROKEN" (not just bent), it is very hard for you to forgive because you give so much in return. Your writing is bold, clean, full and if Aquarius the bottom letters are wide and optimistic as the "t" is crossed very high and long.

There are many "sciences" that correlate to each other and that do not correlate to each other as well. The main thing is to be open minded and educate yourself to all the different ways we communicate and it could actually be very beneficial to you.

There are multiple stories written/told by very successful people on how they either consciously or unconsciously use these sciences every day…especially successful negotiators, salesman and councilors. How?

Well, by knowing what makes a person tick, or seeing that trophy fish picture on the wall gives you the "ice-breakers," you need to get your foot in the door for them to listen to you.

All you have to do is keep your communication tools open to perceive all the positive notes the universe is playing for you to "hear."

TEACHER told us this many times and in many different yet the same way…it is "difficult communicating with a rock but once you have the rock's attention the universe opens up."

ET-BEINGS' OTHERS' COMMON EYES

IG Sloped up

"Normal ET-BEING'S Modified Cat-Tipped Eyes"

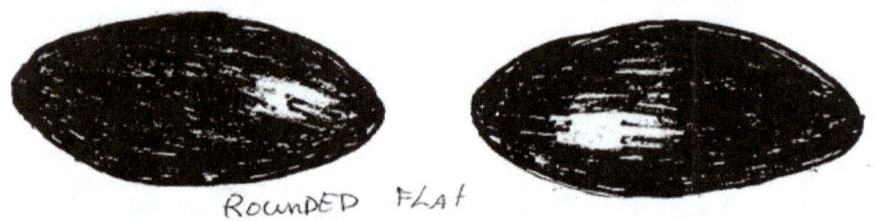

ROUNDED FLAt

Rounded Oval Wider Bridge Eyes

Round FLAt BAT EYES

Modified Slanted Barrel (Common Reptilian)

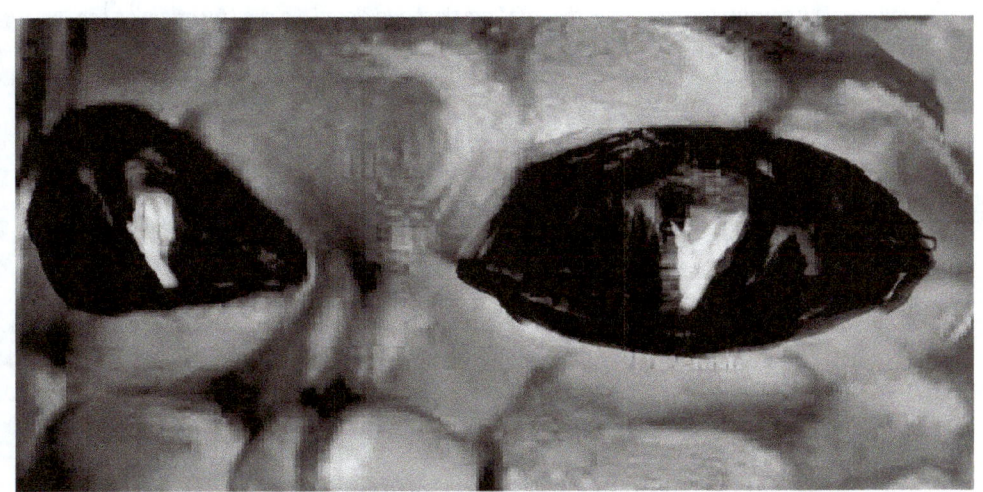

OTHER SPECIES (REPTILIAN NOT DRACONIAN), These are actually "semi-friendly," compared to some OTHERs. I think way back in TEACHER's past and our future, I think these were who got called GREYS that actually helped the androids/cyborgs with the DNA mixtures and also we "councilors" to the humans undergoing the transformation from human to becoming an ET-BEING. The emotional, physical, spiritual and mental trauma/HELL the humans endured to try to make sure that man-kind survived above all else requirements.

NOTE: ALL ET-BEINGS and OTHERS were called devils and demons by the religious orders.

More Face reading and "opinion" information:

Below are some human common jaw lines and explanations:

NARROW JAW LINES:

This aspect of human and ET-BEINGS species such as TEACHER and her kind are very similar as in the need to try to avoid discord or aggressive acts by others. The strong desire to negotiate (either verbally/telepathic) a mutual understanding is very desired. In order

to resist or counter act others to "control you" you make the decision to often give in believing it is your decision and what is best for all.

Opinion: if your star/sun sign is Aries or Virgo the giving in to others could often be due to constant need for attention as in "bad attention is better than NO attention." Your handwriting will reflect this conflict if the "t" is weak, low or very little crossed...if the "a/o" are tight and closed the need for attention can sometimes be over-whelming and cause personal and/or emotional conflict. This emotional conflict can make many psychiatrist happy as they know you are going to be a long paying customer...because they will label you (female or male) "Histrionic and/or Bi-Polar."

JAW   Lives
HUMAN

NARROW

WIDER

HUMAN

WIDE JAW LINE SHAPE VERY PROMINENT (Especially in Male/Female)

NOTE: If the jaws are visible from behind (hair missing) then these traits can be even more pronounced and definitive.

You are a natural born fighter when it comes to inner strength and the word quit is not in your vocabulary. Regardless of the odds against you...you will keep plugging away until the foe is too worn down to do anymore battle. This can cause you to be very self-sacrificing and injurious to yourself.

Opinion: If your star/sun signs are a Scorpio, Aquarius, or Capricorn this self-sacrificing warrior soldier determination can get you killed especially on the war combat battle field. However, it can also save your butt and your fellow soldiers as well because you fight beyond the odds. If you cross your "t" high wide and strong even more fight. If the "g/y/j" and bottoms of the "f" are wide then you give and take full-heartily.

RIPPLED JAW LINE ESPECIALLY IN BACK NEAR EAR AREA (USUALLY ONLY MALES)

THIS COULD BE A VERY PHYSICAL INDICATOR OF REPRESSED ANGER AT ANOTHER/ GROUP OR EVENT THAT YOU HAVE NOT COME TO GRIPS WITH AND A "PEACEFUL" UNDERSTAND/ACCEPTANCE. THIS REPRESSION CAN BE DISPLAYED IN VERY UNHEALTHY PHYSICAL AND MENTAL ABUSIVE WAYS TO YOURSELF AND OTHERS.

Opinion: If your star/sun sign is Leo, Scorpio, Aries, realistically all this can be very damaging to your health...worse in Leo, Scorpio, and Aries. The "repressed EXPLOSIVE personality" can be "calmed" but you have to "internally" choose to want to lose the need for your repressed anger and "mentally" wipe the slate clean for whatever reason you feel the repressed aggression. If your handwriting is sharp, quick, jerky, disjointed and you dig into the writing surface or you beat the crap out of the keyboard (no medical physical disease)... please do yourself and all a peaceful jester and seek understanding...remember this is just my opinion and there is NO proof by anything that I say that makes it true...just correlated observations.

NOTE: ROUNDED AND RIPPLED ALIEN JAW LINES ARE NORMALLY REPTILIAN AND/OR DRACONIAN STYLE SPECIES. THE NATURAL RIPPLE SCALES OR OVERLAPPING SCALES ARE THE "NORMAL" APPEARANCE OF THE OTHERS THAT FALL INTO THOSE CATEGORIES. THE REPTILES HERE ON EARTH ARE VERY SYMBOLIC OF THAT SKIN/SCALE PHYSICAL PROFILE AS WELL AS THE MENTAL INHERENT ACTIONS AND INTERACTIONS WITH OTHER SPECIES THEY CONSIDER INFERIOR...OR AN ABSTRACT VIEW OF FOOD.

AS I ELUDED TO IN MY DIFFERENT BOOKS THERE ARE OTHERS THAT ARE NOT GREYS NOR TERRESTRIAL ET-BEINGS. WHAT DO I MEAN BY TERRESTRIAL ET-BEINGS...THOSE LIKE TEACHER AND HER KIND?

"TERRESTRIAL ET-BEINGS" LIKE TEACHER AND HER KIND NORMALLY ASSIGN THEMSELVES TO THE "MILKY WAY" GALAXY AS WE CALL IT. TEACHER AND HER SPECIES DEFINES IT AS THE HOME CLUSTER. HOWEVER, THAT HOME CLUSTER HAS BILLIONS OF STARS AND PLANETS WITH OTHER SPECIES ON THEM. THAT DOES <u>NOT</u> MEAN THAT "OTHERS" FROM DIFFERENT GALAXIES DO NOT TRAVEL TO OUR HOME CLUSTER AND BEYOND. WE ARE SO IGNORANT AND UNQUALIFIED TO KNOW/UNDERSTAND JUST WHAT IS OUT THERE!

MAYBE WHEN TEACHER AND HER KIND ARE OFFICIALLY ANNOUNCED, ACKNOWLEDGED, AND APPRECIATED FOR WHAT THE FUTURE HUMANS DID FOR PRESENT DAY MAN-KIND...MAYBE WE WILL BEGIN TO BE QUALIFIED TO KNOW THE BASICS OF THE UNIVERSES.   I AM NOT GOING TO TRY TO HOLD MY BREATH THAT LONG!!

Chin Line / shape
ALIEN

NOSES REMEMBER WHEN GRANDPA GRABBED YOUR NOSE AND PULLED OFF YOUR FACE? I really don't know a lot about noses and personalities that I personally trust as in nose shapes and behaviors compare.

I've seen some very narrow noses that are supposedly have very empathy for others especially if narrow nostrils that are pointed because you are often seen as very conservative when it comes to money and sharing and as I said I've known these people to be very giving and mentally and financially supportive of others and that includes people they don't personally know as in charities etc.

Opinion: sun sign cancer and rising in Leo are the only ones that may have this behavior. However if the "a/o" are wide or open they are usually more generous, and if the "y/g" is wide this is even to the point they give away money too freely

ALIEN NOSE

short/short

short/narrow

Long/narrow

Long/narrow

ALIEN LIPS

Thin/Short

Thin/Long

Average Full

Thin, Short, DOWNWARD

Thin, Long, DOWNWARD

HUMAN LIPS

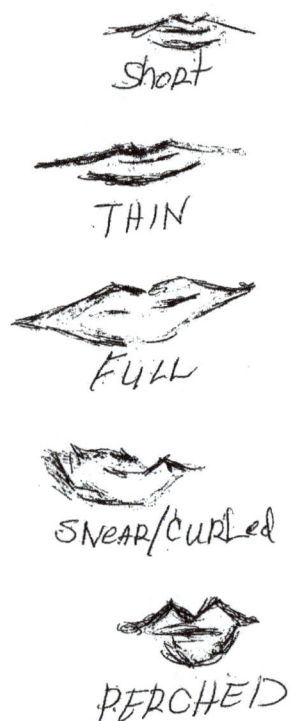

Short

THIN

FULL

SNEAR/CURLed

PERCHED

ALIEN FOREHEAD

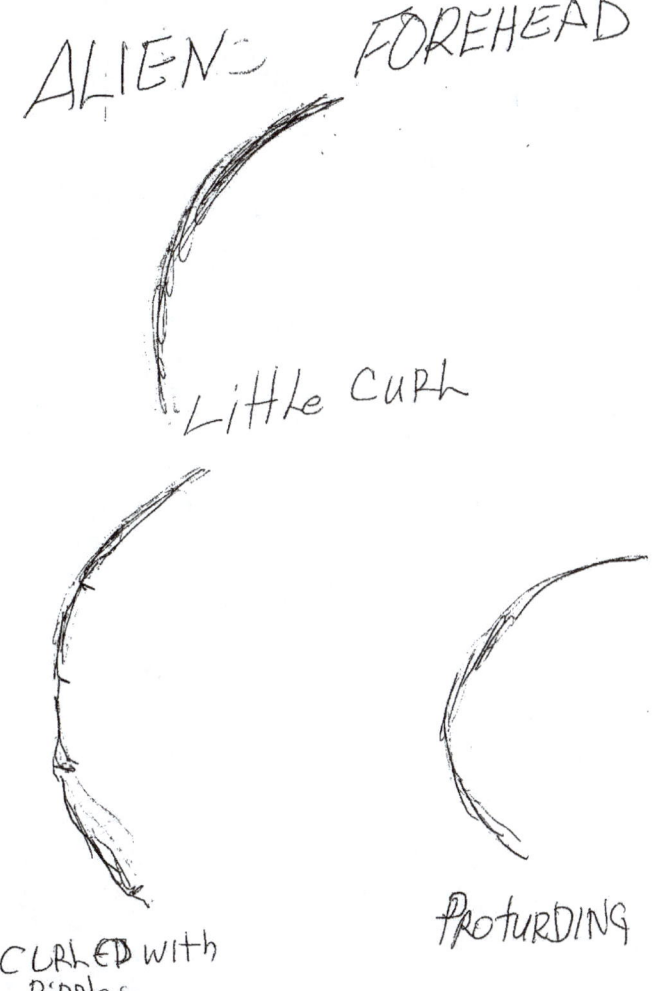

Little Curl

CURLED WITH
Ripples

PROTURDING

HUMAN FOREHEAD

SLOPED BACK

No shope

Rippled/Lines

I purposely did not write anymore about people's faces and
correspondences to "aliens." The correlators are too far apart

especially since the aliens are primarily cloned which screws up the normal processes of evolution which is principle in reading and interpreting human faces.

This even goes into the art of reading the body gestors etc. Humans and space beings are so very different especially in association with a non emotional being and an emotional being.

I just wanted to give you some food to chew on as in just "stewy" knowledge.

But WHAT IF the space being can alter itself to look like grandma?

WHAT IF????

****

TRANSPLANTEE JULY 10, 1856

Who died 70 years later on probably the same day he was conceived on a cold winter's night in his mother's/father's bed?

It is rumored in the old records that he was about a month early and his mother was very concerned about his birth. This rumor is only implied in one old record of his family. His father a strict minister said it will be GOD's will what happens to the child.

So, how could this child be a "transplantee," if he was one?

On December 19, 1855 there was a massive freakish "meteor show." Why freakish because there were no known meteor activity scheduled during this time of the year. There was a lot of religious consternation because this was close to Christmas and the end of the world and Christ is coming and all kinds of hooey bluey stuff was being spouted.

Well, meteors that strike the earth are called meteorites-correct? Well, some of the flaming meteorites were impacting the earth all over the place, and this actually got logged and catalogued as a "UFO sighting of strange lights." Don't believe me…check the newspapers!

What has to happen for a transplantee to be "created?" Yep, an ET-BEING has to give up its spirit before the human spirit takes control of the human fetus. Well, there are some very cold nights/days in what we call Yugoslavia where it is even too cold for the vampire out very far away from a warm fire back in its spooky castle. And this is when our person was conceived...about 3 weeks before this freakish meteorite bombardment to place.

You guessed it. One of these flashy meteorites was our Kamikaze ET-BEING. When the ET-BEING staged his fiery entrance and impact that is when the transplantee was created. And he would grow up into a normal European home until adulthood to become a very famous inventor who because of his spirit's agreements and his star sign and his sun/moon/Jupiter were is negative square with each other he was destined to be in very emotional battles that often were to his detriment, and also make him very prone to strict OCD behavior...even to the point of paralyzing him to "function in public."

Also remember, this person is designed to operate on a 9 volt spirit battery, but because his spirit was an ET-BEING he was running on 12+ volts every second of his life. Even in the womb which may explain why the rumor was he was born about a month sooner that mother/father and the mid wives though.

He was a brilliant student in school and after achieving advanced education levels especially in math and science he moved to America to make his life there. He eventually got a job in the Edison factory.

This is where he and Edison often butted heads on how electricity should be produced and used. This long bitter feud even lead to the death of a fully grown elephant as Edison demonstrated on Jan.4,1903 in public how his rival's electricity was very dangerous and deadly. The elephant smoked and burned while horrified lookers watched the animal twitching, long dead from being severely electrocuted. However, he beat out Edison at the Chicago World's Fair by lighting the entire complex and also creating the first hydro-electric power station from Niagara Falls in New York. These events drove Edison into deep seclusion.

His laboratory in New York "mysteriously" burned to the ground taking many of his very valuable patents and patent papers with it in the fire. There were rumors that Edison was a "poor loser." Just ask the dead elephant if he is or not!

Soon with a lot of money from JP Morgan he moved to Colorado Springs and set up a massive "free energy" project there and perfected his name sake coil. After years of very vivid experimentation and show and tell projects even to people like Huck Finn/Tom Sawyer author and many more "nice to know" celebrities when he actually had JP Morgan convinced he would deliver free electricity to the world JP Morgan pulled the support and tore down the 130 huge tower because…there were going to be NO power meters that Morgan could charge since he wanted the energy to be FREE!

About this time Marconi plagiarized and stole his radio patents and took credit…later the Supreme court gave him back his patent but not the NOBEL Prize that Marconi stole from him. A lot of that history is not in the history books like it should be and nor are the inventions that he created the Edison tweaked and took credit for as well.

However, before his death he had amassed 494 patents to his credit and was a pioneer in many of the products we use world-wide today and will use far into our future.

Even though he was profoundly OCD with eating, silverware and many other "rituals" he never married and never ever really got the recognition and gratitude he deserved while he was alive.

Was he a transplantee…you tell me if you have ever thought that **Nicolae Teslea** (no middle name), was a transplantee or not?

Oh, it is strongly rumored that his lab was totally striped down to the floorboards and the museum only got "items" that had been very public and everything else was carted away and is stored in a safe secure bunker, somewhere by THEM that don't exist, and wear very dark large sunglasses even in the inside.

WHAT IF Tesla lived just ten more years…what advancements would we have today that is child's play…would we have fully functional AI robots that are FREE care givers?

WHAT IF???

* *

When is **AGOD** not **OGOD**:

 I wanted to make sure since this book seems to be spilling the beans
on a lot of subject that…No, TEACHER I did not make a mess for you to
clean up, and the cat is still in the house, basking in the afternoon
sun by the patio door!

As stated before seeing stuff from TEACHER and many of her kind and
similar is tricky and it requires an in-depth understanding of the
basics of ET-MATH as introduced and briefly explain in other ET-
BEINGS books.

Look at the simple example below. Viewing on way gives the
observation point a very different point tan the "Actual object
center of observational mass point.

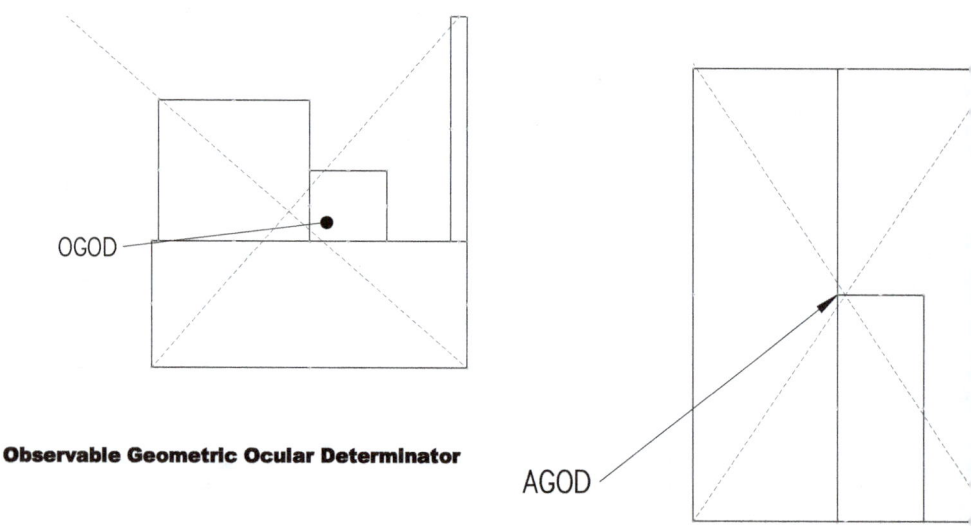

Observable Geometric Ocular Determinator

Actual Geometric Object Determinator

OGOD and **AGOD** determination…demonstrating the actual differences in
the Observable Geometric Ocular Determinator and the Actual Geometric
Object Determinator point

There are some very specifics that need to be understood if you want to understand the basics of ET-Math and/or how the ET-BEINGS species see objects that use the large stereoscopic inner/outer eye configuration.

1). The OGOD is always going to be predominantly on the outer surface especially when being view from anywhere that is NOT perpendicular to "0" degrees top (Zenith) or "180/0" degrees bottom (Nadir).

2). AGOD is always viewed from max Zenith or max Nadir.

3). Remember in space Zenith and Nadir are NOT always on the vertical as they are here on earth. Gravity "differentiationates" vertical from the horizontal more expressively by the curvature of the planet...not true in space.

4). ALL dimensional dimensions (inch, yard, mm, meter, etc., etc.), are expressed in degrees. That is why the pi (3.14 eastern and 3.14 x.011) Mayan), is universal. Unknown to either east or Mayan the true pi of 3.14 for east and Mayan is divided in half and that is the UNIVERSAL pi number. There are so far over a million integers...I am NOT going to list them here however, IF 3.141592653589 as indicated by Univ. IL (100,000 places of pi web site were converted to the true Universal it would be 3.14159275459 and that is the pi (10 million digits) x D (degrees) = Circumference...

5). This is the beginning of understanding the visual 6 dimension X/Y/Z viewing plane.

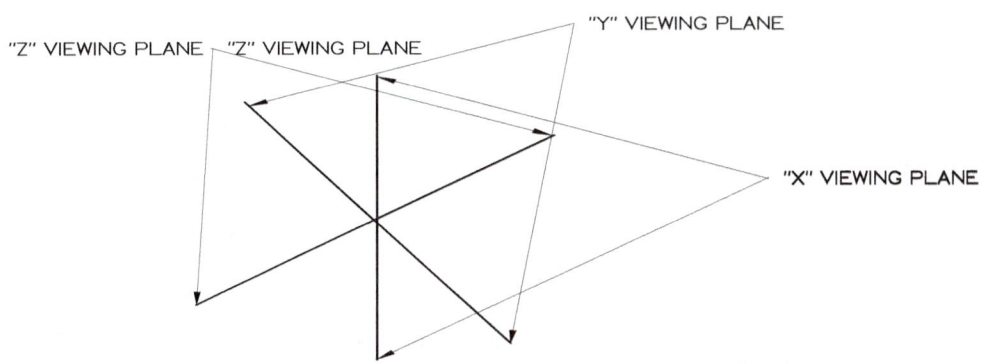

Get yourself a good stiff drink before reading this....

1). Anywhere along line "X" is a viewing point. The absolute edge is called "X Minimum" and the total opposite side of the line is called "X Maximum". The edges are so minute that even a sub-atomic particle can not fit on the edge without "falling-off." This law holds true for all the other lines as well. These XYZ "intersecter lines" are always 90 degrees to each other, no matter what degree the primary line is. Who/what is the primary line...you decide that. (I told you get a good stiff drink).

2). Each viewing plane from the center (XMin XMax X .5), is always 1/6th of the area circle/sphere regardless of how long/short that line is. Each line can be an infinite number of spheres. (sure you don't want that drink...well, I do). Maybe a drawing or two may help.

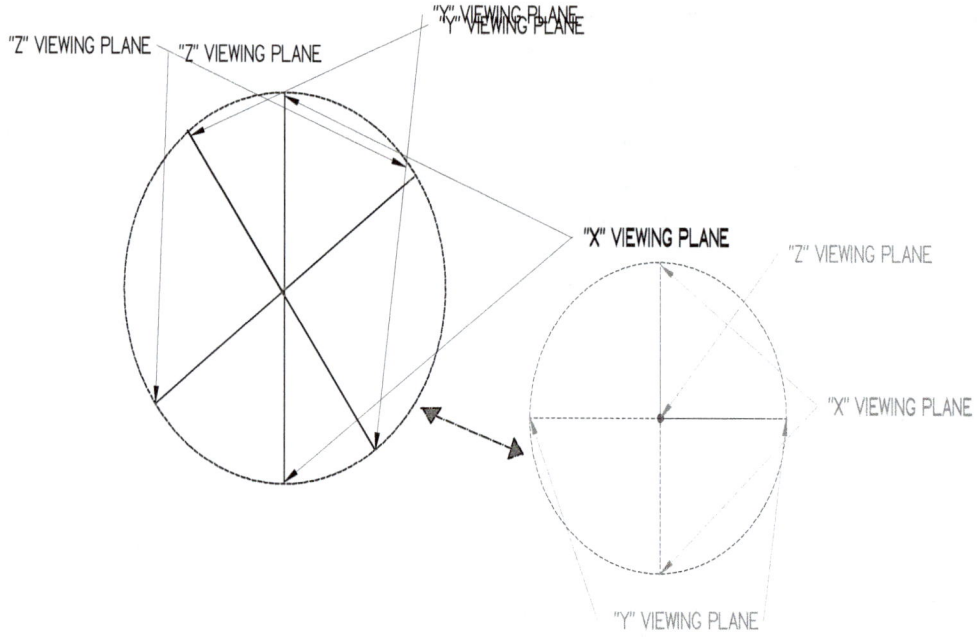

All joking aside as I stated each section of an axis center point is 1/6 of a sphere or a 60 degree area on a 90/180 degree line/plane. Also anywhere upon that line can be a viewing point and from that viewing point to one "edge" can be any degree between 0—180 or any portion of a degree. Remember that statement as it is very important. You have drawings to help you understand that better.

The drawing with the perpendicular vertical/horizontal cross members with a prominent dot. Realize the dot is also a perpendicular intersecter line to the other two lines. Thus it can be any of the three axis lines. In this example the dot is the "Z" axis line.

The dot is also a 0—180 degree axis that the center point is 90 degrees perpendicular to all the other 5 segments of the sphere. Thus it is the 6th segment of the sphere as well, and all six segments are perpendicular to each other thus making a (IMPORTANT STATEMENT HERE--), MINIMUM OF 6 FULL DIMENSIONS WITHIN THE VIEWING SPHERE. Therefore, the 6 full segments can be ANY combination of 6 dimension degrees.

The area of the circle is pi x (rxr=r sq)…however that is NOT the area of a sphere…and it sure is not the volume of a sphere that formula is $V = 4/3 \ \pi r^3$ or approx. 4/3=1 1/3 X (3.146 x r x r x r)= V.

That is what TEACHER and those like her brain does automatically as they view objects, interprets the volume in degrees seamlessly…just like we see inverted objects on our retina and the brain flips it back up-right.

Artificial Interpretations/Intelligence and Alternative Reality (ies), even at our very primitive level that we are so impressed by and "blown-away" with all the advanced technologies that we are discovering must realize a minimum of the 6 dimensional viewing and interpretation requirements.

Those symbiotic impressions, expressions, perceptions, and reactance's to Artificial Interpretations/Intelligence and the melding of Alternative Realities is going to require as I stated before the total understanding and freely chosen acceptance of "TRUE Artificial Interpretations/ Intelligence before man-kind can utilized TRUE AI/AR for what they really are and meld safely into man-kind's existence.

I wrote about what TRUE AI is previously. Please review and study how that can be seamlessly molded into present day man-kinds' world. I wrote about it fairly extensive in **ET-BEINGS 5 When You See PREMA You See PRETA.**

True AI/AR integration into present day man-kind is going to require an entire change of present day man-kind mindset. And this WILL go against every GREYS agenda for man-kind reason for existing.

I will try to communicate with TEACHER more about this present day and near future mindset that exist today and the implications to all the players involved in man-kind's ultimate survival.

Until if and when, then it is going to be very interesting to see who comes to the table with open arms…and who/what comes to the table to "eat" us…after-all we are just meat to many predators.

WHAT IF THEY ALL BRING FORKS AND KNIVES TO THE TABLE?

WHAT IF???

* *

TEASER TECHNOLOGY…TEACHER'S BATTERY

First and very important I am NOT BSing you. I 've made this non chemical battery, it works and Still is working. Pay attention here…IT is NOT here…it is NOT anywhere on this planet. TEACHER and her kind have it on their star cruiser for "safe keeping." However, everything I share with you in this segment should allow you to build one and pay my designated heirs the royalties that it and the Margie Generator will produce as in ALL my technologies shared with you in my ET-BEINGS books, DVD, and classes. Since all these technologies are covered by the national and international copyright laws. I want to make sure my bloodline keeps getting the royalties for all my work long after I am no longer on the face of this planet.

That said, Now I am sharing with whomever wants to build my technologies presented to you as I said in all my books, DVDs, and/or classes etc.

Imagine if places like Porter Rico, Philippines islands and several other places around the world had just these two technologies in operation? Here is what I am talking about a TEACHER non-chemical battery bank and a Margie generator in a truck about the size of a 5 ton can supply 100,000 of watts of power in a matter of hours, instead of now days, weeks, months, years, or never. Any power line that is not destroyed in a hurricane and capable of carrying electricity can be tied into the TEACHER battery band and Margie generator.

Guess what since the TEACHER battery virtually never needs recharging you have a portable power source that provides emergency recovery power to give plenty of time for repairs and replacements. There are 1,000s of things to do with batteries that virtually never need recharging...just imagine all the uses we use batteries?

Transient Enveloping Amplified Continuous Hyper Energy Replicator

(TEACHER)

The **Transient Enveloping Amplified Continuous Hyper Energy Replicator (TEACHER)** power unit is a very unique non-obvious invention that utilizes well known laws of science, physics and magnetics to produce virtually an unlimited source of green energy (non-fossil fuel).

The **Transient Enveloping Amplified Continuous Hyper Energy Replicator (TEACHER)** power unit is a very unique design of permeant magnets that attract and repel each other at a specific designed time to move their respective "EDDIES" through a copper tube that is also a copper coil configuration. The eddie's (magnetic field electrons), collect on the copper coil tube producing current/clean energy.

The **Transient Enveloping Amplified Continuous Hyper Energy Replicator (TEACHER)** power unit operation consist of photo-optic switches to rotate the stronger attractive pole, and then reverse to rotate a stronger repelling magnet into position. This action causes the **Transient Enveloping Amplified Continuous Hyper Energy Replicator (TEACHER)** power unit internal magnets to move up down the copper coil tube causing the eddies to be extracted, and collected in the energy collector unit.

The **Transient Enveloping Amplified Continuous Hyper Energy Replicator (TEACHER)** power unit internal magnets are forcibly repelled and attracted by the stronger pole magnetic beta fields to produce faster more eddies and faster repelling/attraction action, within the copper coil tube.

The **Transient Enveloping Amplified Continuous Hyper Energy Replicator (TEACHER**) power unit rotating repelling and attractive magnets are operated by a single pole single throw servo that is initialized by an optic beam sensor when the internal magnet breaks the optical switching beam. The optical switching beam energizes the servo motor switch to rotate either the same pole or opposite pole magnet into position. The rotation of the opposite pole or the like pole is designed to get the internal magnet to move faster up/down within the copper coil tube. This rapid enveloping action of falling and forcibly repelling upward and attracted to the top produces a rapid fire of eddies to be extracted for the magnet beta field, and the collector collects this current. For distribution...in this case to the battery trickle charge unit for the servo motor.

The **Transient Enveloping Amplified Continuous Hyper Energy Replicator (TEACHER**) power unit is unlike any other power production unit, No it is not perpetual motion/energy, however the permeant magnets within the system should be able to provide a designated supply source within itself for a longer period of time than standard power sources (batteries etc.), that needs no recharging like standard batteries do now days.

The **Transient Enveloping Amplified Continuous Hyper Energy Replicator (TEACHER**) power unit is designed to be a stand-alone unit or can be combined in series or series/parallel to produce the green, clean, and long lasting power requirements desired (see drawings).

The **Transient Enveloping Amplified Continuous Hyper Energy Replicator (TEACHER**) power unit detailed operation is based upon specific timing of switching poles to repel and attract the internal magnet.

- The N-52 cylinder internal magnet (1—?). The number of internal cylinder magnets depend upon the length of the coiled tube between the attracting/repelling magnets.

- As long as there's gravity the cylinder magnet(s) utilizes the gravitational force to freely fall towards the plastic base where the non-magnet counter weight is sitting (ferrous metal weight). The ferrous metal causes an acceleration of the falling speed for eddies to be extracted.*

- Just as the free falling accelerated cylinder magnet(s) (groups of magnets represent one extra strong internal magnet) therefore, will be termed as "magnet."

- The repelling/attraction magnet will need to be twice as strong (magnetic beta force field), than the internal magnet. These should be N-52 high grade magnets.

- The falling magnet breaks the optical beam switch causing the servo to rotate one half rotation bringing the extra strong N-52 repelling magnet into position to rapidly repel the internal cylinder magnet while the ferrous counter-weight is moved away.

- At the same time the extra strong repelling magnet slams into position the extra strong N-52 attraction magnet at the top is now adding the attraction force as the repelling magnet propels the internal magnet upwards towards the very top of the copper coiled tube.

- Just as the internal magnet is about to impact the extra strong attraction magnet the optical beam switch is triggered to quickly rotate the attraction magnet to the extra strong repelling magnet and the ferrous counter weight is quickly placed at the bottom of the coiled copper tube.

- The extra strong repelling N-52 magnet at the top slams the internal magnet down the copper coiled tube extracting eddies as it rapidly falls, and is forcibly attracted towards the ferrous counter-weight.

- The rapid falling internal magnet which is forcibly repelled and attracted to the ferrous counter-weight. However, as the optical beam switch at the bottom is broken, and the servo rapidly rotates another one half turn the entire power generation cycle is complete.

- The copper coiled tube collector has collected magnetic eddy electrons and is ready for power distribution.

The **Transient Enveloping Amplified Continuous Hyper Energy Replicator (TEACHER)** power unit is a very unique non-obvious invention of clean green power generation that should prove much more efficient than conventional power sources, and be very adaptive to space powering systems that require longer than standard recharging power periods to operate in deep space as the **Transient Enveloping Amplified Continuous Hyper Energy Replicator (TEACHER)** power unit powers/propels (ionic drive), vessels to the stars.**

The **Transient Enveloping Amplified Continuous Hyper Energy Replicator (TEACHER),** unit for deep space is uniquely designed to function after the power from solar radiance or winds is not effective (presumed to be past Pluto). The closest star outside our sun is Alpha Centauri (distance of 4.37 light-years (1.34 pc ...25 trillion miles), and about 8 billion miles before the on-board solar power systems would start to be activated by Alpha Centauri's suns. Those in-between miles of no power from solar etc., would render the deep space probe inoperable and frozen in a very deep freeze condition.

The **Transient Enveloping Amplified Continuous Hyper Energy Replicator (TEACHER),** unit if designed as a deep space probe presently being considered to have a nuclear power reactor system to provide power for deep space exploration. This type of power system for deep space exploration has many drawbacks in addition to the known expected continuous power production capabilities.

The **Transient Enveloping Amplified Continuous Hyper Energy Replicator (TEACHER),** unit offers many options for power production that does not exist on the open market today. These options could open up a vast amount of technology development opportunities from non-recharging batteries for cars, security monitoring systems, emergency disaster power replacement, isolated security for DOD locations, and many more uses in addition to power deep space exploration without the dangers of radioactive reactors dangers.

The **Transient Enveloping Amplified Continuous Hyper Energy Replicator (TEACHER),** unit offers disaster recovery of power a lot faster especially when tied in with the MARGIE generator as mentioned in other PPA. These two systems together can be tied into existing power lines capable of transporting power in a matter of hours instead of the usual long delays experienced presently. And since the TEACHER battery bank system requires virtually no recharging the recovery time is greatly shortened and made more effective to relief needless suffering/discomfort, possibly death from improper medical care or food production.

*Note: in non-gravitational environments the alternating repelling of like poles, and the alternating attraction un-like poles will provide the oscillation that produces traveling eddies.

TEACHER power unit designed for deep space internal power production far from standard solar or battery power production capabilities in use presently.

The **Transient Enveloping Amplified Continuous Hyper Energy Replicator (TEACHER),** unit can be used virtually anywhere we need battery power.

Now Kiddies I am going to tell you step by step how to make a TEACHER Battery...Don't ever say I did not help/give you anything...As I said in ET-BEINGS 1...I DARE you to tell me where the fiction and non-fiction divide...IF IT does. I also said, my ET-BEINGS books DVDs, and classes will be unlike any others, and I am making good on my promises in everything I present to you.

IF not.... then _**PLEASE PROVE ME WRONG**_!

Here is step by step how to make a TEACHER Battery and remember it is copyrighted and me and my heirs get the royalties if ANY of my technologies are produced to commercial level...and IMHO if you don't make them then what can I say, when you are given gifts, it's polite to say THANK YOU.

TEACHER Non-Chemical Battery Power Production Unit

The TEACHER Non-Chemical Battery Power Production Unit construction process is not very complicated in relationship to the reliable longevity operational capability.

Prototype model: Wear Protective items including eye protection... these Magnetic configurations can crack and explode propelling shrapnel pieces with a lot of force

• Decide on the size of the cylinder magnet to float up/down inside the copper tube on its eddies'

• Decide on the size of the copper tube based upon the size (OD), of the cylinder magnet

• DANGER: Use a wooden dowel to allow the cylinder magnet free-fall towards the strong repelling magnet (make sure the repelling side is up and can not flip as it could crack and explode upon impact with the other magnet) The taller the protective plastic tube surrounding the wooden dowel and cylinder magnet from the strong repelling magnet the better as the repelled magnet could jump higher than anticipated. The plastic tube should protect/prevent the cylinder magnet from striking the repelling magnet and give an accurate height reaction indicator/position

• The height must be documented to give you an idea of the repelling height when the cylinder magnet is within the sealed copper coil

• 16 gauge solid copper wire is wrapped around the copper tube making a coil (number turns varies)

• Ends of the copper coil are not bent but point straight from the ends so caps fit over ends

• Before testing any repelling/attraction magnets at the ends of the copper tube test the falling rate of the cylinder magnet within the copper tube

• Next test the falling rate of the cylinder magnet within the copper tube with the copper coil surrounding the copper tube

• Next attach the red lead to one end of the coil, and the black lead at the other end of the coil and set the meter on 2 volts DC

• Drop the cylinder magnet within the copper tube and monitor the fall rate along with the voltage produced as the falling cylinder magnet falls within the copper tube

• Next remove the copper tube and monitor the fall rate of the cylinder magnet within the coil without the copper tube

• Monitor the falling speed and the voltages produced from the falling magnet within the copper coil

- Note that the meter range may need increased to accurately record the voltage since the magnet is probably falling much faster thus producing more current/voltage

- Note the differences of the fall rates and the voltages produced

- Attach the clear plastic resting shelf at the bottom with tape and glue making sure it is very secure

- Next mount the most efficient configuration on the stand and attach the repelling rocker arm mechanism in position (see drawings to help with determining location etc.)

- The bottom of the coil/plastic shelf should be just as close to the repelling magnet surface as possible without touching the repelling magnet surface when it is flipped into repelling position.

- During installation with all the above mentioned parts insure that the internal cylinder magnet is free to rise and fall as the magnetic force affects its direction of travel

- Securely attach the clear plastic shield at the top where the rotating attraction magnet with flip into position

- Note: as long as used in an earth gravitational environment there is no need for a repelling top magnet as gravity will provide significant falling speed. If the unit is used in a non-gravity environment such as outer space then the rocker arms will need an attracting and repelling magnet to provide active forces against the internal cylinder magnet

- Set the repelling/wait magnet detection switch to automatic speed on the optical activated control circuit

- As the cylinder falls it breaks the optical switch, flipping the strong repelling magnet into position

- This repels the internal cylinder magnet back up inside the coil

- The strong repelling magnet instantaneously moves out of position allowing the internal cylinder magnet to free fall again until it breaks the automatic optical control switch, and the process begins all over again

- As the repelling magnet moves into position so does the attractive magnet at the top adding additional height/distance force advantages acting upon the internal cylinder magnet

- The TEACHER Non-Chemical Battery Power Production Unit, will produce energy every time the cylinder magnet moves up/down within the copper coil. The amount of power is based upon distance and speed the cylinder magnet moves within the copper coil

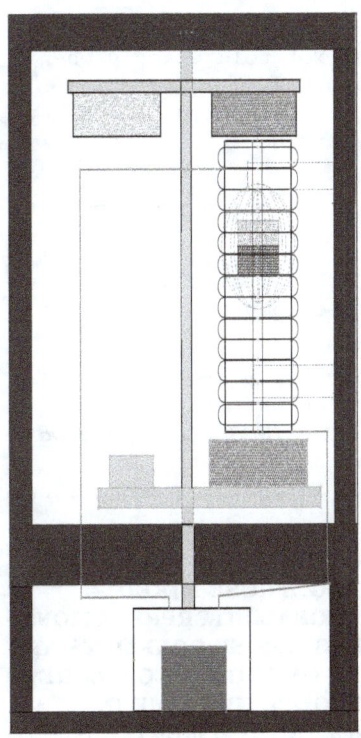

The motor at the base rotates the repelling/drawing magnets as the optical switches are triggered by the rising/falling N-52 magnet(s). Non-gravity the top magnets are stronger to compensate for no gravity.

Remember it works, I built it, and tested it, and it still works and is with TEACHER and her kind for safe keeping...PS TEACHER's battery has been working for over a 1,000 years, and I plan on powering PREMA/PRETA with a TEACHER Battery bank system.

WHAT IF You make a TEACHER Battery and/or a MARGIE generator

WHAT IF???

****

Conversations with TEACHER............

Many weeks later....

TEACHER and her kind have been doing "documentation" work in other areas and also preparing for a meeting. I am Not told exactly when that meeting will take place but, I understand they will offer support before the big asteroid is projected to not strike earth but, do a LOT of atmospheric and planetary damage around 2086...give/take a few years one way or another.

I explain that range of dates in more detail in my **ET-BEING WORLD** classes.

Never-the-less, I did get in contact with TEACHER and I "did not beat around the bush" either asking her some very serious cold hard fact questions...such as...

*TEACH I have many deep questions that revolve around the mindset of humans, the survivability of humans, the development of True AI and/or AR, the diseases (as talked about in **ET-BEINGS 1 A Report On Extraterrestrial Communications**), the natural solar events that threaten earth, the misinterpretations of the Mayans, and other stuff as it "craped up" during our conversations.*

WE PERCEIVE YOUR CONVOLUTED BRAIN WAVES AND UNDERSTAND THE CONFLICTS THAT YOUR THOUGHTS ARE PRODUCING. THOSE MIXED THOUGHTS ARE INACCURATE DUE TO YOUR EMOTIONAL INTERPRETATIONS OF FEAR AND CONCERN OF YOURSELF AND OTHERS. THOSE CONFLICTS ARE GOING TO MAKE UNDERSTANDING AND ACCEPTING OF LOGIC A LOT MORE DIFFICULT FOR YOU. THAT WILL PRODUCE NON PRODUCTIVE TIME IN UNDERSTANDING AND ACCEPTANCE OF THE CONCERNS YOU MENTALLY PRODUCE AND WILL REQUIRE MORE THAN ONE COMMUNICATION EVENT TO MODULATE YOUR QUESTIONS AND CONCERNS. YOUR PERSONAL DATA HISTORY IN THIS AREA IS UNCLEAR AND LIMITED.

TEACHER since you realize that I have so many convoluted concerns that are modified by emotions, what am I supposed to do in order to understand what you are saying in a non-emotional perception?

THE EMOTIONAL INFLUENCE YOU HAVE AS A HUMAN I HAVE NO MODIFIER TO MODIFY YOUR LOGICAL PERCEPTIONS NOR REACTIONS. THE CHOICE AS YOU SAY IS A FREE WILL YOU WILL NEED TO SUPPLY TO THE UNDERSTANDING AND ACCEPTANCES OF THE INFORMATION PROVIDED.

Okay I think I understand what you are saying. The not being an emotional human is going to be very difficult for me to develop, and modify into my reasoning abilities.

WE AS ONE UNDERSTAND THE CONFLICTS. IMPUTING DATA TO YOU WILL BE FACTUAL THEREFORE LOGICALLY THERE WILL BE NO NEED FOR EMOTIONAL ANALYSIS OF YOUR PERCEPTIONS. WE WILL NOW ANSWER THE FIRST QUESTION THAT WE PERCEIVE FROM YOU.

THE GREYS ARE OUR SPECIES SUPERIORS AS THEY ARE SUPERIORS TO MANY OF THOSE THAT WE ARE AWARE OF. THE QUESTION ARE THEY TOTAL SUPERIORS WE HAVE NO CONFORMATIONAL DATA THEREFORE WE CAN NOT MAKE THAT STATEMENT. AS TO THE NEGATIVE ENERGY THAT GREYS REQUIRE THE HUMAN ALONG WITH MANY OTHER SPECIES AND EVENTS THROUGHOUT ALL THE UNIVERSES, TIME REALMS AND DIMENSIONS PRODUCE THE AMOUNTS NEEDED. THE QUESTION THAT THE NEGATIVE ENERGY THE HUMAN PRODUCES IS FACTUALLY NON ELEMENTAL IN SCALE TO THE TOTAL NEGATIVE ENERGY PRODUCED. THE LOGICAL ODDS ARE YOU AS A HUMAN ARE NOT EVALUATED AS A REQUIRED PART OF THE PRODUCTION.

TEACHER are you saying even today that all the negative energy that the human produces now is not even a measurable amount to the GREYS' negative energy needs?

YES.

So, my concerns that if we develop a "peaceful True AI and/or AR platform" that will not cause the GREYS to want to remove the human because the production of negative energy is no longer there?

YES, AS SAID THE NEGATIVE ENERGY PRODUCED BY THE HUMAN RATIO IS IN-CONSEQUENTIAL TO THE GREYS NEEDS.

Logically there is no need to eradicate the human.

LOGICALLY, NO

But…

YOU ARE REACTING TO THE EMOTIONAL DOUBT. STAY WITH THE LOGIC

That's easy for you to say. You and family have had eons practice to do what you are asking me to do. If I can look at this stuff 50% less emotional than I would normally react to, I personally feel like I am doing pretty damn good.

YES, IT IS A FACT THAT WE AS ONE HAVE HAD LONGER EXPOSURE TO BEING EMOTIONLESS AND AS YOU KNOW THE EMOTIONLESS BEHAVIOR IS A PREFERRED BEHAVIOR THAT NEEDS TO BE UNDERSTOOD.

Well, actually the information does make me feel a little more comfortable that we are not going be on the GREYS' radar for termination.

YES, IS THAT NOT A LOGICAL ASSUMPTION BASED UPON LOGIC?

Yes to your double logic speak...logically I am concerned with your lack of documentation.

YES TO YOUR LOGIC BUT NO TO YOUR STATEMENT AS WE DID NOT STATE WE DID NOT HAVE DATA ON GREYS' BEHAVIOR. WE STATED IN REGARDS TO THE LACK OF YOUR DATA INDEPENDENTLY.

So you are saying your data on GREYs' is what logically says man-kind has very little to worry about being terminated especially, if we produce less negative energy by producing a positive mind-set towards true AI and AR.

YES BUT THERE ARE MULTIPLE CHANGES THAT DATA RECORDING DOES NOT PRODUCE NEGATIVE ENERGY. THE ENERGY THAT YOU ARE USING IS DRAINING ON YOUR ABILITIES AND WE WILL END THIS SESSION IN A SLOW DRIFT BACK TO YOUR DOMICILE.

Thanks TEACHER, I am sort of tired and I'm realizing I am in my recliner rocker on my screened-in porch.

YES, YOUR LOCATION IS TRUE AND YOU WILL SOON BE THERE INTACT.

Thanks...I need to talk with you more...much, much more, soon.

YES, SOON

Man, I love my glider rocker. It is so smooth and comfortable especially when there's a nice, clean, and cool breeze coming in from the east (ocean). Plus the screen keeps just about all the bugs out and Fred and Ethel (two lizards), and I sleep on the front porch. I have no idea if FRED and Ethel are male/female one is just smaller than the other so I know which is which. However, Ethel "dares" me to get as close as I do to her so I don't know if she is male or not...however she/he is more defiant of "big giants," on two legs and a beer in one hand and a ham sandwich in the other. I bet it's the ham sandwich, and not my "magnetic personality."

Three days later...raining like a cow pissing on a flat rock! I am in my recliner in the house as the wind is blowing rain all over the porch and my outdoor glider.

TEACHER are you summoning me?

YES   THERE IS NO LOGIC TO YOUR QUESTION   YOU CAN NOT GET ELECTROCUTED
BY LIGHTENING BY TELEPATHIC COMMUNICATIONS. TELEPATHIC COMMUNICATIONS
DOES NOT PULL IN THE FREQUENCIES THAT WOULD ATTRACT LIGHTENING
CHARGES, ESPECIALLY IN A DOMICILE AS YOURS WITH GROUNDED CINDER BLOCK

Just checking I don't want any shocking surprises.

WE DO NOT PRESENT ANY FACTS THAT YOU WILL BE ELECTRICALLY SHOCKED

*TEACHER, you said last time that there is very little need for
concern that the human would be terminated because of man-kind
changing its mind-set from so much negative energy to more positive?*

NO, TO NEED FOR CONCERN AND NO TO YOUR QUESTION. THE AMOUNT OF
NEGATIVE ENERGY YOU PRODUCE IS ONLY A SIGNIFICANT PART OF MAN-KINDS'
LIFE PROFILE, AND ANY CHANGES AS YOU PERCEIVE AS POSITIVE OR NEGATIVE
IS ONLY SIGNIFICANT TO THE HUMAN, IT IS NOT SIGNIFICANT TO THE GREYS.
THEREFORE, LOGICALLY YOUR MISGUIDED EMOTIONAL ASSUMPTION IS IN ERROR.

*Good that makes all of me, myself and I feel better for this being
and all other human beings. What about you and your role and
responsibility to ensuring man-kind survives?*

THE PRIMARY MISSION IS TO PROVIDE DETERRENCE AND PROTECTION FOR THE
HUMAN BEING TO SURVIVE. WE AS ONE HAS DONE THAT BY OUR ALTERATIONS.

*TEACHER! That is not fair! You know damn well I mean for man-kind to
survive as an advancing human in physical and technological advances.
You and your kind have expressed the undesired outcome of your
alterations as you put them…but it is what YOU and YOUR KIND have
become. Are you saying that is the ONLY way man-kind will survive is
to become like…………no-offense LIKE YOU!*

THERE IS AS YOU SAID NO OFFENSE THAT IS EMOTIONAL AND DOES NOT
PROVIDE ANY SIGNIFICANT SEGMENT TO THE OVERALL MISSION REQUIREMENT.
OUR ALTERATIONS HAS ASSURED THAT OVERALL MISSION REQUIREMENT IS
ACHIEVED AS WE AS ONE ALTER OUR EXISTENCES THROUGH EACH ADVANCED
CLONING PROCESS.

WHY DO YOU WISH I CONSUMED ALCOHOL?

*Because Teach, I could use a very stiff drink about now…and I need to
logically non-emotionally understand and accept that man-kind
survives as you….Screw it I am getting that damn drink like it or
not.*

LIMIT IT TO NO MORE THAN 2.5 OUNCES OF 90 PROOF SO YOUR BRAIN WAVES
ARE NOT AS YOU SAY MUDDLED.

Teach, I'll sip as we talk…I like to enjoy the flavor of good bourbon and conversation with a good cigar, but I have not smoked in over 56 years and it was only a pipe and a few rum soaked cigars then. It's funny how you still miss the flavor of something so long ago.

THE ANALOGY IS THE SAME WITH US AS ONE EVEN THOUGH THE EMOTIONAL IS NOT THERE THE REMEMBRANCE OF THE PHYSICAL STILL IS PRESERVED IN THE DATA RECORDS.

LOGICALLY AS YOUR NEED FOR CONCERN IS VIRTUALLY NIL, THAT EQUATES TO OUR AS ONE AWARENESS NEEDS ARE ON THE SAME LEVEL AS YOURS. AS YOU AND I DISCUSSED BEFORE, OUR IN ABILITY TO MENTALLY BOND WITH THE GREYS IS OF NO CONCERN BECAUSE WE CAN MELD WITH THE HUMAN AND WE WILL KNOW WHEN THE HUMAN IS BEING MANIPULATED. THAT FACT ELEVATES THE NEED FOR NO CONCERN.

TO ANSWER YOUR QUESTION OF MASKING. THE HUMAN BRAIN IS SO PRIMITIVE THAT MASKING AS YOU SAY OR HIDING IS NOT POSSIBLE BECAUSE THERE IS NO PLACE WITHIN THE HUMAN BRAIN TO HIDE THE MESSAGES FROM OTHERS.

Are these others in addition to the true GREYS?

YES.

So you and your kind know when "Others" are…………

YES, WE KNOW WHEN OTHERS ARE AS YOU ASK ABDUCTING HUMANS AND OTHER CREATURES WE CAN MELD WITH. OUR INTERACTIONS ARE NOT AS CONTROLLING AS OTHERS ARE. LOGICALLY BECAUSE OUR ANCESTORS WERE HUMAN WE ARE LOGICALLY MORE AWARE OF THE HUMAN PSYCHE AND MENTAL LIMITATIONS WHEREAS OTHERS ARE AWARE BUT LESS INFLUENCED.

Are the others the ones who really do a lot of emotional and physical trauma to humans?

THAT IS AN EMOTIONAL QUESTIONS AS TO THE LOGICAL SEVERITY TO A HUMAN IS DIFFERENT IN EACH HUMAN AS YOU WELL KNOW YOU ARE DIFFERENT AND RESPOND DIFFERENT THAN OTHERS. THE AMOUNT OF TRAUMA AS YOU SAID IS AN INDIVIDUAL ACCEPTANCE OR REJECTION AND UNDERSTANDING OF THE ENCOUNTER PROCESS.

Teach you know damn well I mean the Others are more aggressive and less aware or caring in the abductions/encounters.

YES.

Then you and your kind get blamed for a lot of bad stuff in these encounters.

YES.

But you do medical documentation and probing and that same stuff as well.

YES, THERE IS AN AWARENESS TO MODIFY FEAR INTENSITY WITHIN THE INTERACTION

To be totally honest with you TEACH, the fear that I remember honestly was within myself as I did not know what these strange looking beings were going to do to me. My fear made my actual encounter actually a lot worse than the actual encounter was. I remember voices in my head saying to be calm. It's funny you'll laugh at this (if you laugh), I remember to this very day when I was very young and I peed in my under-ware how warm it felt; and I'll be damn if that feeling didn't make me feel better…then the table I was on felt warm, like I had peed a flood on it and I felt more relaxed.

I REMEMBER THOSE DATA RECORDS AND YOUR INNER ABILITY TO BE ABLE TO COMMUNICATE REGARDLESS OF YOUR EMOTIONAL FEARS AT THAT VERY YOUNG HUMAN STAGE OF DEVELOPMENT. YOUR CONDITIONING AT YOUNG YEARS AND YOU CHOOSING TO FREELY UNDERSTANDING AND ACCEPTANCE OF MENTAL COMMUNICATIONS IS WHAT FACILITATES OUR ABILITIES TO COMMUNICATE PRESENTLY, AND AS LONG AS YOU PROCESS THOSE CAPABILITIES WE WILL BE ABLE TO COMMUNICATE VIA MENTAL INTERACTION WITHOUT THE POSSIBLE NEED OF PHYSICAL INTERACTION.

My family always said I was weird.

YOUR INDIVIDUAL SPIRIT UNIQUENESS PROVIDES THE CONDUITS TO TELEPATHIC COMMUNICATIONS

Is that another way of saying I am weird?

THERE IS NOT ENOUGH DATA TO MAKE THAT LOGICAL ANALYSIS

Understood

DO YOU WANT TO TERMINATE THE COMMUNICATIONS SINCE YOU SEEM TO BE IN A BALANCED STATE OF MIND?

TEACHER, that would actually be very agreeable as I would like to analyze the contents of our conversations especially in regards to subjects I think I want to talk about with you next time.

THAT WOULD BE AGREEABLE TO US AS ONE AND WE KNOW WHEN THIS MEETING WILL BE IN YOUR FUTURE BUT FAR IN OUR PAST. HOWEVER, AN EVENT OR TWO WILL COMPLICATE OUR NEXT MEETINGS.

WHAT! What events?

WE WILL NOT DISCUSS BECAUSE AS YOU WELL KNOW THIS WILL ALTER THE EVENTS AND THE IMPACT…NO IT IS NOT DEADLY TO YOUR SPIRIT.

Man what a way to leave a cliff hanger.

MOUNTAINS ARE NOT IMPORTANT TO YOUR EVENTUAL EVENTS.

I'll make sure I do not travel near any mountains and stay in the valleys.

Several weeks have passed and there were several events that happened not only to me but to a large portion of the planet as well. So, one evening it was nice and there was not much traffic on the street so TEACHER contacted me with a question. As I said, Normally I am the one with all the different questions but her question was actually an answer to some of my questions.

WE WILL ASK YOU A QUESTION THAT LOGICALLY ANSWERS A SIGNIFICANT PORTION OF YOUR CONCERNS. WHY IS YOUR EARTH WITH ALL OF ITS DIFFERENT EMOTIONAL DIFFERENCES THAT ARE SO SEVERE THAT THEY CAUSE WAR HAVE AGREED ON HOW TO DENY OUR KINDS' PRESENCE?

That's not fair Teach, hitting me with such a blockbuster like that before we even get settled down into the glider and I had a sip of beer yet. WOW! I am sinking down in the soft cushion and sipping my beer before I even try to answer that.

THAT IS ONE OF YOUR CONCERNS YOU HAD BUT WERE HAVING DIFFICULTY EXPRESSING TO YOURSELF AND TO WE AS ONE.

TEACHER, let me ask you this…are the governments of each of these world- wide countries…are they the only one making the rules?

NO TO THE MAKING YES TO THE ENFORCING THE AGREEMENTS.

Crap! Teach I can understand this better IF I though or sort of knew it was the "governments" who made the rules and enforced them too. However, what you are saying is that someone or something tells the governments what to do and how to do IT!

YES

Okay, sister do YOU know who IT is!

NO AND YES TO SOME OF YOUR QUESTION. NO I AM NOT A SIBLING NEITHER FEMALE NOR MALE. NO WE CAN NOT PERCEIVE THE COMMUNICATIONS OF THOSE IN THE DECISION MAKING PROCESS. YES THERE ARE MORE THAN ONE SPECIES

THAT TRAVEL THE UNIVERSES THAT WE CAN NOT COMMUNICATE WITH IN ADDITION TO THE ONES YOU IDENTIFY AS GREYS.

Can't you read the humans' and learn who or better WHAT is communicating to the humans?

NO THE DECISION MAKERS ARE AWARE OF OUR ABILITIES TO DO THAT AND ALL COMMUNICATIONS TO THE GOVERNMENTS ARE VIA ELECTRONIC SOURCES THAT WE AS ONE AND MANY HAVE NOT BEEN ABLE TO INTERCEPT.

What about…

YES WE AND OTHERS HAVE GONE AS FAR BACK IN COMMUNICATION TECHNOLOGY AS TO WHAT YOU CALL MORSE CODE, BASIC MACHINE LOGIC, ANALOG, DIGITAL, BINARY, LASER FIBER OPTICS AND EVEN MORE ADVANCED THAT YOUR PRESENT DAY HUMAN HAS NOT PERFECTED THE INSCRIBING AT THE ATOMIC AND SUB-ATOMIC LEVEL.

So you buzz the White House/Capital building every once in a while like in 1952. 1963, and missile silos and take them off line etc., just to get the humans' attention.

YES, WE AND OTHERS DO THAT AND MUCH MORE TO ACCOMPLISH OUR MISSION OBJECTIVE.

Let me take a good swallow before I ask this question in the most logical way my pissed off brain can muster.

YOU ARE CONVOLUTED

Damn Right I am Convoluted! But…

I WILL ASSIST IN FORMULATING YOUR QUESTION IN LOGIC. YES THE HUMAN IS VERY AWARE OF US AND OTHERS. YES THE ACKNOWLEDGED SIGHTINGS, ENCOUNTERS AND VISITS ARE DRAMATIC INCREASE AND SO ARE THE NON-ACKNOWLEDGE EVENTS AS WELL ALL DESIGNED TO GET MAN-KIND AWARE OF US AND OTHERS. YES YOUR GOVERNMENTS ARE DEFENSIVENESS AGAINST OUR AND OTHERS TECHNOLOGIES. AS YOU KNOW WE ARE NON-AGGRESSIVE AS OTHERS ARE. YES, YOUR HISTORY HAS HAD MANY TOTALLY DISRUPTIVE SOCIAL CHAOS EVENTS. HOWEVER, THE LOSS OF CONTROL OVER THE POPULACE WOULD BE WORLD-WIDE AND THE DATA RECORDERS HAVE NOT RECORDED ANY SIGNIFICANT EVENTS OF OUR OR OTHERS ACCEPTANCE.

So as far as the world general populace is concerned you and your kind do NOT exist.

YES, TILL WE AND OTHERS ARE ACCEPTED

So, you and your kind do everything you can to make sure our sorry asses survive, and we the present day human does everything we can to makes sure you are totally denied of your existences or acceptances?

YES, AND THOSE THAT ARE IN THE DECISION MAKING PROCESS.

What a bucket of shit…

WE UNDERSTAND YOUR LOGIC AS A BUCKET OF WASTE HAS NO VALUE

Yeah something like that.

Since more than 90% of the world's population says or say you are real and believe you exist what happens if the people start demanding the truth?

WE HAVE NO DATA RECORDED OF THAT. THERE IS MASSIVE DATA OF HUMANS' LIVES BEING KEPT CONTROLLED BY COMPLEX, CONVOLUTED, POLLUTING EVENTS THAT PRODUCE YOUR WARS AND MANY OTHER WORLD-WIDE DISASTERS THAT THE PEOPLE NEVER ACCORDING TO DATA RECORDS DEMANDED THE ACKNOWLEDGEMENT AND ACCEPTANCE OF US, OUR KIND OR OTHERS.

That's a barrel of shit!

AGAIN AS IN NO VALUE EXCEPT AS ORGANIC FERTILIZER

Okay TEACHER I got one for you that is as pure logic it can be coming from a human rationalizing brain. IF all the 100,000s even millions of "eye-witnessed" accounts are denied and rebuffed as hooey delusions etc., then would IT NOT be Logical that the very most important damning evidence in court is the "eye witness account" why is it courts of law that even have judgment on life and death the "eye witness testimony" is considered so reliable especially if the person testifying has a high ranking in society such as police, firemen, pilots, doctors, lawyers, teachers, you understand right?

YOUR QUESTION AS LOGICAL IS VERY EMOTIONAL DRIVEN AND I AS MANY SAY THE EMOTIONAL AND LOGICAL WANTS AND DESIRES OF THE HUMAN IS VERY COMPLEX AS TO WHAT IS WANTED AS REAL AND WHAT IS SAID TO BE WANTED AS REAL. OUR DATA BANKS ARE VERY FULL OF THESE EMOTIONAL LOGICAL CONFLICTS WITH THE HUMAN BEING SPECIES.

Are you actually saying be very careful for what you wish for, because you might get it and it is not what you thought it would be like?

YES. EACH HUMAN HAS TO DECIDE INTERNALLY WHAT THEY WANT AND WHAT THEY WILL FREELY ACKNOWLEDGE AND ACCEPT WITHOUT CAUSING INTERNAL DURESS.

Is that why your data recorders have no or very little history of that happening?

THERE IS NO SIGNIFICANT AMOUNT OF INFORMATION TO LOGICALLY EVALUATE YOUR QUESTION EITHER IN THE AFFIRMATIVE NOR THE NEGATIVE PARAMETERS AT THIS SESSION.

So you and your kind go on with the mission while the whole world is being programmed to deny you and your kinds' existence.

YES TO THE MISSION NEEDS. THERE IS INSUFFICIENT DATA FOR THE LATTER PART OF YOUR QUESTION.

You know what TEACH?

YES, YOU NEED A WHAT YOU CALL A TIME-OUT MENTAL BREAK.

Yes, and a very strong drink so I will not muddle or screw up or worse our conversations.

AGREE

Later TEACH

I am sunk deep into my glider rocker on the front porch listening to the sounds all around me, and I am actually too weak to get up and go have that stiff drink. Damn I need a servant robot who knows how to make a double Black Russian...what I need is a sex bot that is a damn good bartender, too.

Later............

Hi TEACHER how has the Universe been treating you?

THE UNIVERSES HAVE NO EFFECT ON OUR STATE OF BEING OTHER THAN WHEN SAFETY PRECAUTIONS ARE NOT TAKEN.

Okay...I have written down some questions so I can remain as unemotional as possible but I feel these are very real logical questions that need answers

First, TEACHER what do you hypothesize which is stronger the governments or religions?

FACTUALLY, THE RELIGION AND GOVERNMENTS OF A COUNTRY ARE VERY CLOSELY RELATED AND THE HYPOTHESIS THAT ONE IS STRONGER THAN THE OTHER IS A RELATIONSHIP OF PRIORITIES OF THE TWO FACTIONS AND THE PEOPLE IN THE DECISION MAKING PROCESS OF EACH SEGMENT OF THE FACTIONS.

That does not answer my question...who has more control?

AS STATED FACTUALLY, THE RELIGION…

Who has more power and exerts more control of the people in Europe?

RELIGION IS A VERY STRONG INFLUENCE ON THE HUMAN BEING LOGICALLY MORE THAN JUST EMOTIONAL AS IT MELDS INTO THE SPIRITUAL REALM AS WELL. GOVERNMENTS ARE FACTUALLY MORE DISARRAYED DUE TO CHANGES OF DECISION MAKER POSITIONS WHEREAS RELIGIONS ARE CARRIED DOWN THROUGH GENERATIONS.

Is that true in all countries?

YES THAT WOULD BE A LOGICAL PREDICTOR.

Just what I thought…

Who has more real estate value?

THE GOVERNMENTS LEASE MORE FROM OTHER TITLE HOLDERS. LOCATIONS THAT ARE USED AND ARE NOT USED BY GOVERNMENTS ARE HELD BY GOVERNMENTS FOR GOVERNMENTS AND OTHER NON GOVERNMENT ENTITIES USE.

Are you placing parks and national monuments and other places like that in that statement along with what we call government buildings or non-public sites like military bases and stuff?

YES.

What religion owns more real estate?

YOUR ANSWER IS COMPLEX AS IN MANY OF HUMAN'S RELIGIOUS ORGANIZATIONS ARE FORMULATED UNDER DIFFERENT LAWS. WHAT IS PRESENTED AS A CHURCH OR PLACE TO WORSHIP IN ONE AREA IS NOT ACCEPTED IN ANOTHER. THIS RELATES TO YOUR MANY RELIGIOUS SPIRITUAL CONFLICTS OF HARMING AND KILLING OTHERS. WHERE ONE RELIGIOUS ENTITY IS RECOGNIZED AS A COUNTRY UNTO ITSELF THE NEIGHBOR SEES IT AS A PLACE OF DECEIT AND EMOTIONAL, PHYSICAL, MENTAL AND SPIRIT MISERY. YOUR EARTH HISTORY HAS SEVERAL DOMINATE OLDER RELIGIONS DOCUMENTED IN THE DATA HISTORY FILES. THEY ALL STRIVE FOR CONTROL OF OWNERSHIP OF TANGIBLES INCLUDING PEOPLE AS PEOPLE ARE REPRODUCES AND CONSUMERS.

TEACH why is it that I think I have generated some very simple logical questions and answers and you make a book out of each question that produces a lot more questions?

FACTS AND LOGIC ARE NOT AS EASY TO DISGUISE AS EMOTIONS

Touché' you got me there.

So help me with my next question…what do I need to ask?

YOUR EMOTIONS ARE COMPLICATING THE REASONING PROCESS I FACTUALLY CAN NOT ASK YOUR QUESTION AS IT IS OVER-LOADED WITH EMOTIONAL MOTIVATORS AND THIS IS CAUSING THE CONFUSION TO YOUR REASONING AND QUESTION.

Okay, you mentioned that there are some really old religions…umm Jewish and the Roman Catholic Church. Which one owns more stuff?

DATA REPORTS THAT THERE IS NO INDIVIDUAL ROMAN CATHOLIC CHURCH. RECORDS STATE THE TITLE DOES NOT EXIST. THE VATICAN IS SEEN AS THE RECOGNIZED CORPORATE OFFICE OF THE ROMAN CATHOLIC RELIGION. HOWEVER, BOTH ARE TOTALLY SEPARATE AND NEITHER HOLDS A LEGAL TITLE. EACH CATHOLIC CHURCH IS A BUILDING UNTO ITSELF AND OWNED BY THE VATICAN. THE CORPORATE VATICAN IN RELATIONSHIP TO JEWISH TITLES OF PROPERTY IS THE MOST MONETARY VALUE. AS IN BOTH RELIGIOUS DOCUMENTS HAS PROPERTIES THAT GOVERNMENTS LEASE FOR USE OR NON-USE.

I am surprised I would think China with all its over-populated land would own the most?

THE CHINSES HAVE MANY RELIGIONS THAT ARE NOT AS CONCENTRATED AS THE JEWISH, ISLAMIC, CATHOLIC RELIGIONS. TRUE TO THE MOST POPULATED BUT THAT DOES NOT FACTUALLY EQUATE TO REAL ESTATE HOLDINGS IN THE WORLD.

Again TEACHER do the religions make the rules or do the governments?

LOGICALLY AT THIS TIME THERE IS NOT ENOUGH FACTUAL INFORMATION TO MAKE THAT OR NOT MAKE THAT A FACTUAL STATEMENT.

Okay illogically let's bet what would I have better odds on all the information you have, even that stuff not shared with me that religions make the rules? Would I have better odds on that statement or governments make the rules?

ILLOGICAL AND LOGICAL ARE A CONTRADICTION OF INFORMATION THEREFORE THE ODDS ARE NIL IN EITHER CASE SCENARIO.

Damnit TEACH answer the damn question…be my damn bookie and take my bet!

EMOTIONALLY, PHYSICALLY AND MISSION NEED I AM INCAPABLE OF DOING THAT.

Fine I'll make my own Scientific Wild Ass Guess (SWAG)…and I bet I do not get struck by lightning or go to hell for my guess either.

Are you going to answer any of the questions I've written down or are you just going to confuse me more with your damn logic evasive non-committal answers?

LOGICALLY WE AS ONE WOULD SAY YOU ARE TOO EMOTIONALLY CONFLICTED TO CONVERSE LOGICALLY

Yep, I agree with you…let's just close and we can meet sometime soon when I am not so convoluted as you say.

Damn…Holy Shit! Good… there are no clouds in the sky tonight, not much chance of getting struck by lightning.

****

STRIPPING OFF THE EMOTIONAL FACADE

Now that I have some of your attention by that title let's go full balls to wall and present several LOGICAL **WHAT IFS** that pull no punches and ask some questions that not going to be easy or comfortable to answer.

Let's say the first **WHAT IF** is that TEACHER and her kind all land at the same time or the front lawn, rock yard, sand patch, kremlin or T square and a few other here or there government places of every president, prime minister king/queen and powerful dictator etc., at once, all at the same time day or night.

Let's also say **WHAT IF** they land in front of the Vatican, the "wailing wall, some big mosques, Buddhist temples and any other well-known religious hang out.

Let's say **WHAT IF** TEACHER and her kind block every cellular, satellite, GPS transmitter world-wide at the same time.

In other words **WHAT IF** every computer chip became inoperable at the same time

WHAT IF we passed a law that would supposedly reduce gun violence considerably by declaring a UN law that all hand guns, rifles etc., in other words all weapons must have a computer chip that allows the weapon to work was blocked. And all weapons without the modifications were destroyed except for a few that were smuggled and black marketed but 99% of all weapons were destroyed that did not have the computer chip that authorized use.

WHAT IF we could not get our jets into the air to bomb our own soil.

WHAT IF we could not launch any of our missiles as demonstrated several times at many nuclear missile bases to strike our own white house capital lawn?

WHAT IF no nation's military could do anything aggressive against the visitors except sling shots, rocks and may be a few MaloToff cocktails?

WHAT IF there were no streaming movies on TV , no way a kid can have his face buried in the Ipad for hours, and no talking refrigerator telling you left the damn door open and the light was still own, and definitely no blinking microwave timer.

WHAT IF TEACHER and her kind all landed at once and said, "What's for dinner? You sent us an invitation on the Voguer plaque and here we are. We don't have very strong teeth so we hope you have lots of different soups as we traveled a very long way to get here."

WHAT IF that event going to organized religion and the control it has on the people? OOOPs we are NOT the only dudes in the Universe and WHAT IF the Great Creator was not talking to the angels when he said (if he/she IT did), Let us create man in our own image.

WHAT IF he was talking to TEACHER and her kind?

Realistically think… what would or governments do? What would our militaries do? What would our religious institutions do? And most of all what

WOULD YOU DO?

Listen TEACHER and her kind have NO intentions of doing that. But that would be the only safe way they could visit us. If we are totally incapable of attacking them when they visit. But a visit from TEACHER would worse than an unannounced Mother-in-law visit and she is going to be staying you and off course her three precious cats. Oh what's that you're allergic to cats…well thankfully there's "Benadryl."

TEACHER and her kind know we are dumb enough to bomb, nuke and destroy our own soil to keep control of what is left of the survivors. Be it on earth, moon or Mars or wherever we have stuck a flag and colonized.

If there is really no true "The Day The Earth Stood Still" (original movie), where all power (computer chips etc., except emergency medical planes in flight etc., TEACHER and her kind are not going to visit…I can NOT say that about others.

But that block on electricity/computer retaliation ability will have
to last a LOT LONGER than 30 minutes in the movie.

Realistically, how long do you think that block of aggression by man
will need to last to keep TEACHER and her kind safe?

WHAT WOULD BE YOUR ESTIMATE OF TIME???

**WHAT IF TEACHER AND HER KIND JUST SAID THE HELL WITH MAN-
KIND**

AND DROPPED IN ANYWAY AND ASKED IS "IT SOUP YET???"

****

ET-BEINGS 4

Man-Kind's Extraterrestrial Ancestral Transgressions

(MEAT)

Epilog

Did you catch any word change? I am not going to tell you. I had to
quite writing this book here and leave all those **WHAT Ifs** because
there are some THINGS that are not ready to be known, yet. TEACHER,
said I need to be careful in what I say/write because of the
implications are there and the denial is real and the loss or fear of
loss of control is very real as well.

That is why I am not stating anything definite because truthfully
there is not enough factual information to state one way or another.
The truth could be that an entirely new species other than earth or
any that we know about could be making all the rules and all of us
are being guided by those thought waves to see all those strange
lights and weird looking bugged eyed creatures that are not really
there but only in our programmed imaginations.

The controllers could be us, those that have a lot of clout, power
and social positions from generation to generation and unless you are
born in that blood line forget about getting into it. Or it could be
the military being ordered by our governments to act a certain way so
as not to be too aggressive to the people and just keep everything

unknown and in doubt. Or it can be the powerful religions that make the rules have thousands of secret documents buried in caves, basements and whenever of stuff they don't want us to know. Or it could be all of them put together. Or it could be none of the mentioned and it is not even listed in any of the 1,000s of conspiracy theories.

Do you realize how many conspiracies there are out there? Do you realistically think if any organization or group or individual who manipulates all these events suspected the truth is speculated that the information would last very long?

That tells me in ALL of our conspiracies that…

WHAT IF NONE OF IT OR ANYTHING IS REAL???

I LOVE a Good Cliff-Hanger…Don't You? What is in ET-BEINGS 5 When You See PREMA You See PRETA?????

****

Please review this and all the ET-BEINGS 1—5 books, DVDs, classes…on Amazon of wherever works for you…I prefer Amazon (easier to track) and keep tally for teaching gigs etc.

ET-BEINGS 5 When You See Prema You See PRETA is planned to be published soon. Check out the web site www.etbeings.com and my "facebook" for the latest information and special offers.

Thanks for being a Seeker of the WHAT IFS?

Live Healthy and Inquisitively

John Q. Zarr ("Q" as in John "Q" Public)

PS: Hint don't "freak" out dude.

www.ingramcontent.com/pod-product-compliance
Lightning Source LLC
Chambersburg PA
CBHW051304170626
46809CB00004B/1772